The Ring

Serendipity, Indiana - Book Five

by

Magdalena Scott

The Ring

© 2016 Magdalena Scott

ISBN-10:0-9971922-5-9
ISBN-13:978-0-9971922-5-4

Cover Art by Elusive Dreams Designs
Stock Art from DepositPhotos.com

DEDICATION

This book is dedicated to my parents.
They were artists and lovers of the written word, and
encouraged me to explore my own creativity. I continue
to miss their physical presence, but always carry them
in my heart.

ACKNOWLDGEMENTS

The menu for Carla's home-cooked meal
is brought to you courtesy of Patricia Shrum, whose
contribution was chosen in the random drawing
from newsletter subscribers' entries.
Thank you, Patricia, for the delicious possibilities!

Chapter One

I SLOGGED THROUGH the Dublin deluge. Several beautiful days had passed, with just morning fog or a brief shower. But on those days I was indoors, doing fittings and alterations on a stunning winter wardrobe for one of the most famous and fashionable women in Ireland.

My client seemed pleased with her new clothes, and I anticipated more business would come my way as a result of word of mouth advertising. I tried not to wonder how I could handle additional clients.

It was, after all, a delightful problem.

Ireland enchanted me as always, but due to the backlog of work in my little hometown of Serendipity, Indiana, this trip didn't allow for extended sightseeing. One day in Dublin was my only down time; the next morning I would catch an early flight. I cheered myself with the realization that Dublin in the rain isn't less beautiful than Dublin on a sunny day, just beautiful in a different way.

The taxi driver who picked me up at the front door of my hotel was as bright and encouraging as the day was grey. As requested, he drove through the Georgian Square area so I could see the many colored Doors of Dublin, and crisscrossed the River Liffey a few times. Views of, and from, those lovely bridges are breathtaking.

When I said good-bye to my agreeable cab driver, I set out on foot, thankful for my knee-high rubber Wellingtons and hooded raincoat.

As usual I took time to walk, awe-struck, through the Long Room of the Old Library at Trinity College. The Brian Boru harp, one of only three surviving medieval Gaelic harps, is amazing, as are the two levels of floor-to-ceiling bookcases. I think the flyer said 200,000 antiquarian volumes are housed there. In the previous rooms I had taken time to admire pages of the intricately decorated *Book of Kells*.

I had decided to skip the shopping temptations of Grafton Street, for the most part. Wool sweaters, Waterford crystal, jewelry, and books were all favorites, but I didn't need more. Instead, I would stroll through the National Library, National Museum, and National Gallery. I wondered if I would always visit Dublin alone, or if Jared might like it. A trip to Ireland would be a memorable and educational vacation for his kids too.

But that thought was way ahead of any reality.

When my stomach told me lunch time had arrived, I ducked into a nearby pub. The place was dark and crowded, and the barman made room for me by producing the tiniest table I've ever seen—a small round of scarred wood—and tucking it into a corner. He snagged an empty chair and gestured for me to have a seat.

"What'll you drink, dear?"

"Pint of Guinness, please." I peeled off my raincoat, and began to relax and enjoy the ambiance. Several conversations were almost discernible, some in American dialects. Other patrons spoke with Irish brogues, and one pair of older gentlemen at the bar had such thick accents I couldn't make out a single word. I decided they were speaking Gaelic, the official language of the land.

Grey haired, broad shouldered, and wearing sweaters they may have had for years but which would have cost a mint to replace, their presence made the cozy pub all the more picturesque.

A waitress appeared with my drink, and I ordered a lunch of fish and chips just as automatically as I had requested the Guinness, without looking at a menu. *When in Rome...or Dublin...*

I couldn't stop watching those two older men and wondering what they were saying. They certainly had plenty to talk about.

When my food arrived, I asked the waitress for a glass of water, which I knew would arrive in a chilled glass but without ice. I took a bite of flaky, battered fish and sighed with pleasure.

Sensing that I was being watched, I looked up and caught the two old men looking straight at me.

"Poor dear," said Man Number One. "You're

looking a wee bit lost."

His friend nodded in agreement.

While eating, my mind had slid from Dublin to Serendipity. I chewed and swallowed, set down my fork. I love meeting new people, and was intrigued by these two. It would be fun to chat. "Oh. I'm...I was just thinking." I did *not* look lost, but why quibble?

"Aaaah," they said in unison.

"Thinking of the boy back home who broke her heart," Man Number One suggested to his companion.

Man Number Two surveyed my face again. "No, that's not it. The boy back home doesn't have marriage on his mind." He paused, considering me again. "Or, he has marriage on his mind, but the lady isn't interested."

Number One took a drink from his heavy glass. "Could be he broke her heart *because* he doesn't have marriage on his mind."

I laughed, grateful for their humor. "Okay, you can stop guessing. Not that it's any of your business."

They smiled and nodded. "True enough," Number Two said.

I thought for a moment, deciding whether to joke with them or to be honest and hear the advice they looked so eager to impart. I often find it easy to talk to strangers when traveling, knowing the conversation will be forgotten when we part.

"To set your minds at ease, I'm not heartbroken."

Number One shook his head. "Oh, now there's good news. There's nothing better in this wide world than marriage between two loving hearts, miss."

Number Two clapped a hand on Number One's shoulder. "And nothing worse than loneliness. That's the truth of it."

These gentlemen were too much. "I'm not lonely. I have a busy career, wonderful family and friends. I'm very blessed."

They both looked confused. Number One asked, "You're not planning to marry the fellow then?"

I shrugged, disinclined to get into specifics. Though I hadn't admitted the existence of a man in my life, I also hadn't denied it.

With some painful effort, Number One slid off

his stool and came over to me. "Arthritic, I am," he said in answer to my sympathetic wince. "Doesn't pay to live in a wet climate when old *Arthur* comes to call. But this is my world and all, it is. Wife says let's sell out and move to Arizona." He laughed, as did his companion. He held out his hand. "I'm Mick, and me pal here is Jamie."

I shook his offered hand which did indeed have some knots on the joints. His clothes carried a pleasant aroma of pipe tobacco.

"I'm Carla. It's nice to meet you gentlemen. Arizona is beautiful, Mick, but if you've never experienced summer there, you might want to check that out before moving."

Mick shook his head, watching me. "Won't happen. It's just something the woman mentions when I have my worst days. She doesn't like to see me suffer, and more than that, doesn't like to hear me complain."

Jamie had walked over too, and after shaking my hand he pounded Mick on the back. "Maeve is an angel to stay married to the likes of you all these years."

"As is your Mary, and that's the God's truth."

Mick chuckled back at him. Then his attention returned to me. "This boy-o of yours, Carla. Is he after making you his wife?"

"So far, we're just dating. And, our relationship is...complicated."

Mick held up his hands in surrender. "Ah. Americans and their complications."

Jamie winked at me. "Young people and their complications, you mean."

"Just what is keeping your hearts separated?" Mick asked.

I had asked for this, by letting myself be drawn into the conversation. "A few things, I suppose. He has children. His wife died—"

"Oh! Saints preserve us," Jamie said, with his hand on his heart. "The poor children. They'll be needing a woman in the house."

I sipped my water. "Their father seems to be doing fine at single parenting."

Both men rolled their eyes.

"It's impossible to say where our relationship is going." My voice had grown softer as I spoke.

"You don't care for the children?" asked Mick.

"Yes of course I do, but—"

"The man isn't good to you?" asked Jamie.

"Yes he is, but—"

Mick pierced me with clear brown eyes. "I don't understand the problem."

I looked around, as if anyone else in the place was interested in the state of my life. "For one thing, I'm not like Patty, his first wife."

"Are you supposed to be like Patty, now? Is that what they're telling you?" Mick's bushy brows threatened to unite in disapproval.

"They haven't said that in so many words, no. But when they talk about her..."

Mick interrupted. "Ah, lass, when they talk about her they're trying to keep the memories alive. It's been a little while, I'm guessing?"

"A couple of years."

Mick nodded. "Talking about her keeps her image in their minds. They need to sit and talk about photos, where they were taken, who said what just before the shutter clicked. It's all they have of her, you see. Photographs. The things she touched. As time goes on, Patty may seem all the more perfect to them. It's easier to let any ill feelings go, and forget shortcomings, once a loved one has died. Maybe you're not willing to endure that, and be the person who is only human, doing her best in the here and now."

He was right, wasn't he, that as time passes, it's natural to venerate a deceased person? If I was feeling insufficient in comparison with Patty now, would I find the shadow of her memory easier or harder to deal with in the future?

Jamie drained the last of his pint. "That's something to think about. If you feel you're competing with a ghost, there's no winning."

Mick looked at Jamie. "Still and all, the girl's in love. That much, at least, is clear." Mick's gaze shifted to me again. "It's no wonder you're looking lost, dear. 'Tis a hard thing to know how to proceed with a man who's suffered the loss of his wife."

I pleated a paper napkin, beginning to regret this soul-baring conversation. "I'm old enough to know the challenges." I had never been married, had dated my share of losers, and was more qualified to dump guys than to stand by them. But in theory I knew how healthy relationships worked.

"Hmm. I think you're trying to convince yourself." Jamie shot a mysterious look to Mick, who paused, glanced at me, and nodded.

"Carla, this is meant to go to you," said Mick. He reached into his pocket and withdrew a small, manila envelope which he handed to me.

Weighing nothing, it felt empty, yet Mick's sparkling eyes showed he was eager for me to see what was inside. His attitude piqued my interest, and I opened the envelope with care, in case there was a valuable paper of some sort hiding within. Once the flap was open, I tipped the envelope over my other palm, and a small Claddagh ring slid into my hand. I recognized the traditional Irish design, featuring two hands (representing friendship) holding a heart (representing love) and above the heart, a crown (loyalty).

I met Mick's sparkling brown eyes. "It's lovely. But why do you say it's meant for me?"

"Humor an old man." He paused, taking the envelope and depositing it onto the miniature table. "There's meaning in a Claddagh, you know."

I nodded, examining the delicate gold ring. There seemed to have been an inscription at one time, but it was illegible now. "I've read some about these. Worn on the right hand, with the heart pointed a certain way, it means you're looking for a man. When the heart points opposite, it signifies you're taken. On the left hand, it shows you're either engaged or married. Right?"

"A knowledgeable young woman!" Mick nudged the smiling Jamie before asking me, "And you've a respect for tradition?"

I nodded, still not certain about accepting the ring as a gift.

He leaned closer. "What about magic? How do you feel about *that*?"

My breath caught. "Magic?"

"Nothing dark. I'm talking about the fact that I found the ring in this very pub, one year ago. I turned it in to the barman and he kept it in the lost and found box. Today he handed me that envelope, saying since no one had claimed it, the Claddagh is mine. I have no need of it. The women in my family wear their own."

He stopped, watching my reaction. "I'm giving it to you, and here is the reason. Your mind is whirling with possibilities of this man of yours. You don't seem to know if you're looking or taken." He pointed a gnarled finger toward the ring I held. "Wear this on your right hand. Maybe seeing it there, feeling its presence day and night, will help you decide."

Jamie chuckled. "She likely thinks you're touched in the head."

Mick frowned at him. "Perhaps, but love is no business for the sane." He pointed at the ring again. "Would you be sliding it onto your finger, then, Carla?"

I did as he asked, and wasn't the least surprised that it fit.

"You've put it on to indicate you're taken."

I nodded, contemplating the ring.

Mick cleared his throat. "I wish you all the best in life, Carla. Remember, you can use that as an engagement ring and wedding ring as well. Pass it down through your family to do the same if you wish. There's something very special about an item handed from one generation to the next." He patted my hand, turned and headed to the door. Jamie said good-bye and followed him.

Mick's words were similar to what my grandmother had told me when I was a little girl. I looked down at my hand again, and the delicate gold ring glowed up at me. What a shame someone had lost it and not known where to look.

Chapter Two

AS I WALKED down the hall, I saw Jared waiting for me in the arrivals area of the Louisville airport with a hand-lettered sign saying, *Ms. Standish*. I smiled at him, and his answering grin lit my day. When I reached him I sagged into his arms, the paper crinkling against my back as he held me.

"You're not going to fall asleep standing up, are you?" he whispered against my hair.

Slowly, I pulled back. "Maybe. Unless there's something pressing, I'd love to do that."

"You'll want to claim your luggage. Get something to eat. Go home."

"Oh well, I suppose you're right." I put up a hand to touch his face. "I've missed you."

His kiss was gentle but thorough. "I've missed you too, Carla. We all have."

I scanned the area. "Are Katie and Miles here?"

He shook his head. "Nope. They're hanging out with Melissa and Jim until I get you home. Now that everyone is accounted for, let's go grab your suitcases." He took my tote bag and nudged my hand off the handle of my wheeled case too. "Carla, if you're too exhausted, I can take you to the car and come back for your other stuff if you tell me what to look for."

"Oh no, don't worry. I'll function just fine until I get home. Then I'll collapse." We walked side by side down the busy aisle and stepped into the elevator to the lower level. "Since I had that standing cat-nap I feel somewhat refreshed."

Jared chuckled. "It's so great to see you. Hard to believe you've only been gone a week."

I leaned against him as we watched the luggage carousel, my arm around his waist. "It does seem like a long time. Thank you again for picking me up." Having Jared with me right now felt like being home. That must be an indication of some sort. My thumb played with the back of the Claddagh.

A short while later all my bags had been stowed in the back of Jared's BMW and we were on the interstate heading toward Indiana.

"Where do you want to stop for dinner, Carla? It's all about you today."

After taking a look at the car's clock, I leaned my head against the window again. "Hard to believe it's dinner time."

That's the last thing I remember until Jared shut off the engine. I sat up, stiff from the awkward position I had been in. "Oops. I made a face print on your window. Oh! I'm home."

"I'll clean off the face print sometime, or keep it as a memento. And yes, since you were sleeping I decided you didn't care about being wined and dined as much as being tucked into your bed. Am I right?"

"So right. I'm sorry to be dull."

"Honey, you couldn't be dull if you took an online course." He leaned over and gave me a quick peck on the lips before sliding out of the car and assembling all my stuff at the front door.

As usual I was almost overwhelmed by gratitude when walking up the stone path to my little Craftsman-style bungalow. "Coming home is one of my favorite parts of travel." I put my key into the lock and pushed the door open. Jared motioned me to precede him into the living room, and I did, flipping on the light switch. I picked up the tote and before I knew it, the bags were in my bedroom ready to be unpacked.

"I'll clear out and let you rest, Carla. Unless you want me to grab some carryout and bring it out here."

"Are you going for extra points today, Mr. Barnett?"

"Absolutely. Is that a problem?"

My thumb touched the Claddagh again, a habit that was becoming familiar. "It might be a problem if you get me used to being the center of attention. I could learn to like it, you know."

His face clouded. "I hope you realize how important you are to me. But the kids—"

I closed the space between us, and took his hand. "Jared, I know Katie and Miles are your priorities. I was just being silly, and my joke wasn't funny."

Jared's features relaxed somewhat. "Okaa-ay. So, make the most of the fact that you have me all to yourself." He wiggled his eyebrows.

"You're right. I'd love a pizza from Tony's Macaroni. I've been craving one since leaving Ireland, and none of the Italian places in JFK airport looked as good as Tony's."

"You're kidding again, right?"

"Maybe. But sitting at home eating pizza with you sounds terrific."

Later that evening, we were seated on my patio glider, an empty pizza box on the table behind us. I snuggled further into Jared's embrace.

"Serendipity is so much quieter than Indianapolis was, but being out here on the farm at night is like another world," Jared said. "Besides the restful silence, I'm astonished how many stars are visible without light pollution." He took my hand and sighed, a sound that seemed to indicate contentedness. He raised my hand trying to see the ring. "Is this new? I don't remember you wearing a ring."

I had practiced my answer. "It's a vintage piece I picked up in Dublin." This was as close to the truth as I expected Jared to handle. I felt certain he would scoff at the Mick-and-Jamie story. I turned my hand so I was holding his again, linking my fingers with his, taking the focus off the ring. "Now. Tell me about your week."

Chapter Three

I WAS IN the workroom of my shop, eating lunch with Melissa, my sister-in-law and lifelong best friend. The tasteful lighting was switched off in the showroom of my internationally known dress shop, *Creations*, and she and I sat in our usual spots in the tiny lunch area on the back side of the velvet drapes.

Mel gestured at me with her chicken salad sandwich. "Carla, what's going on with you and Jared anyway? Sometimes I think you're heading toward matrimony, and then—nothing. Are the two of you just torturing the rest of us?"

Everybody in Serendipity knows everyone else's business, and if they don't they might just make up something more interesting than the truth.

"Jared and I are doing fine, Mel. Not everybody is into whirlwind romance, you know."

"I'm not asking for whirlwind, just visible movement. I thought he might say something when he drove up to get the kids the other night, but *nada*. You're going to stonewall me, too?"

"There's nothing to tell. I appreciate you and Jim giving us that time together. It was a lovely evening in spite of being so tired from the trip."

"And your next romantic evening? All work and no play makes for a Carla who...well, works all the time."

I leaned my chin in a hand, still tired even though I'd been home several days. "Gee, ya think? I'm trying to focus on the fact that my name is a big deal right now and loads of business is coming my way. Who knows when that might change? Just one disgruntled customer with a massive social media following could end it all. Or at least change my career from *dressmaker to the stars* into *dressmaker to the Chamber of Commerce dinner attendees*. I love both sets of clients, but the former is doing a nice job of padding my rainy day fund."

Mel's brow furrowed. "I hadn't thought of the fickle nature of people. I can't imagine one of your designs being at the center of a media firestorm, but stranger things have happened. I doubt you could make a living designing for Serendipity women only." She sipped her drink. "But back to you and Jared. Are you putting the brakes on that relationship because of focusing on work, or is it just turning out that way?"

"I am not. Seriously, Mel, give me a break here. I'm still jet lagged, and not in the mood to dissect the Jared-and-me possibilities."

Her eyes narrowed. "If you insist. Then you can spend the rest of our lunch visit giving me the real story about Dublin. And please note how flexible I am about subjects to discuss."

Avoiding her eyes, I fiddled with the ring on my finger, still not used to its presence. "Right. You're so flexible I should call you Gumby. But—nah. I told the whole family about the Dublin trip. You were there."

Mel's eyes zeroed in on the ring. "That was different. I know you can't say everything in front of your brothers at Sunday lunch. Jim, much as I love him, wouldn't be all that receptive to some of the stories I'd most like to hear. And David has a heck of a time paying attention to anyone who isn't Emily."

"True. I wonder if those two will always behave like newlyweds."

Mel grinned, her eyes sparkling. "I certainly hope so."

"Me too."

Mel's face turned serious again. "You're not going to derail me by talking about Emily and David. And don't even bring up Francie's situation. We'll get to her after we're done with you."

Something was up with my sister, Francie, but she wouldn't tell any of us what it was. "Yes, sarge."

Mel stuck out her tongue. "Listen, Carla, you could make this simpler by just opening up. Do you think it's easy, being the only woman on location to help you?"

I chuckled. "No, I suppose it isn't. Shame on Alice for moving to Los Angeles to be with Robert. And double shame on Francie. How thoughtless of her to live in Florida all these years." Much as we tried to avoid it, the loss of geographic closeness made a difference in the emotional closeness. I missed Alice, and worried about Francie.

Mel raised a hand and snapped her fingers a few inches from my face. "I see you getting all moony about the other girls. Get your mind back here, Carla. Tell me what's going on with *you*."

I met her eyes. Melissa can be a bulldog when she's after something, but her intentions are good. She and I have been friends through some very rough times.

I took a long drink of water. "Mel, wouldn't it be nice if you just let me decide how to live my life?"

She looked stunned. "That's crazy talk. I only want what's best for you."

"I realize that. But how about let's assume I can make my own decisions? I didn't push you back into a relationship with Jim, after all."

She smirked. "I was in town maybe fifteen minutes before he showed up in the living room of my new house, having already been introduced to Matthew by..." She tapped a finger on her chin as if trying to recall the event. "Oh let me think, who was it...?"

I burst out laughing, remembering the scene. "That was different."

Mel leaned back in her chair, nails drumming on the table. "Right."

"That was a total coincidence, plus you and Matthew would have run into Jim before long anyway. Pretty hard not to, in Serendipity."

She looked away, a slow smile of happiness threatening to take the edge off the inquisition she was busy administering. We were all thrilled to have Mel and little Matthew in our family, where they belonged.

Mel looked at her watch. "Okay, Carla, you win this round. But only because I have to meet a client in a few minutes." She gathered her lunch refuse and stuffed it into her bag. "Next time we talk, however, you *will* tell me the story of that item that's been on your finger since you got home from Ireland. And how it relates to Jared Barnett."

Chapter Four

THERE'S ALWAYS FUN, and often drama, on the monthly girlfriend conference call with Francie and Alice. We text and chat in between, but our monthly "date" is sacred. After dinner, Mel drove down to my house from the corner of our family's Christmas tree farm where she, Jim, and Matthew live. She probably would have walked except for the weather. September in Indiana can be as hot as mid-August, or as cold as early November. Today it was somewhere in between. Wind and sheets of rain stripped leaves off the few oak and maple trees and blew them everywhere in a hurry. The evergreen trees, which greatly outnumber deciduous on our farm, resembled big green furry aliens, their many arms flapping in the gale.

The storm reminded me of my last day in Dublin, as if I needed a reminder.

The Claddagh clinked delicately on the glass as I poured wine for Mel and for myself. We would attend the girlfriend group support meeting seated at my seldom-used dining table with my cell on speaker.

I tried to relax and pretend the four of us were in the same room. That visualization ended when I heard seagulls crying behind Francie's voice. Evidently one of us was having a nice evening on the beach.

I took a sip of wine and set my glass onto the table. "Sounds relaxing where you are, sis. Having a clambake?"

Francie huffed a sigh into the phone. "I walked down to the beach to watch the sunset."

I—not we.

"I'm sorry, honey. You're okay? And—-Brad?" I put the feeler out there, even knowing she wouldn't open up.

"I'm fine. Nothing new here, but I've been looking forward to our chat."

I nibbled a bit of apple and pushed the plate of

snacks toward Mel. "Me too. Want to be sure everybody's on the line. Or whatever we call it with cell phones. Alice? You there?"

"Yes. It's the middle of the afternoon here in Southern California. Beautiful day. Of course, so was yesterday..." Alice's voice was serene, as it had been since she and Robert got together.

Mel and I looked out my patio doors, which were being pelted by horizontal rain. An occasional tree leaf was plastered to the glass until another onslaught of water removed it.

Mel said, "Alice. Spare us, please. We're having a thunderstorm here that's predicted to last most of the night."

In teenage days the four of us would pour our hearts out to each other. Many were the times we would sit making daisy chains on a hill of the farm, catching up with the latest broken heart and planning our futures.

Alice said, "Since your weather is sucky, I won't mention that I'm sitting by the pool under a sun umbrella, okay?"

Mel rolled her eyes and chuckled. "Right. We

definitely don't want to hear that, Alice." She squirted fake cheese onto a cracker and turned to me. "Take it away, Carla. The troops are assembled."

"I don't have much," I said. "The shop is super busy. My Dublin trip was lovely but tiring."

Alice asked, "You are still seeing Jared Barnett, right, Carla? You know that's what we all want to hear about."

Mel giggled. "If you were here in town, girls, you'd see that Jared and Carla's relationship is moving at the pace of a snail on downers." She waggled her eyebrows at me. "Pick up the pace, Carla. He and the kids are settled into life here, and we all know you and Jared had one of those love-at-first-sight meetings. I highly recommend the married state, girlfriend." She squeezed my hand. "I've never been happier in my life. Neither has Matthew."

Neither had my brother Jim, without a doubt. But my situation was so different from Melissa's.

"Yes, I care for Jared. I'm just not sure..."

Francie interrupted, "What is it that you're waiting for, sister?"

My heart was beating like crazy. "Okay, you're going to give me grief forever on this, but here goes. I'm waiting for a *sign*."

Chapter Five

WITHOUT HESITATION, MEL nodded. "I hear you." She and Jim broke up in their senior year of high school, and the miracle of Matthew helped bring them together two decades later. Their sign had been irrefutable.

"I understand, Carla." Alice had married Dean when they were young. They'd had a long, pleasant marriage that ended with Dean's sudden accidental death. A magical blank book brought Robert, and passionate true love, into her life. She'd gone from reasonably happy wife to sorrowful widow, and now that she had Robert, seemed more alive than ever.

"I don't know, Carla," Francie said slowly. "I get what you're saying, and sure, Alice and Mel had their signs. But I didn't, really. And I'm okay."

Was she? Francie didn't seem very okay to me.

Mel frowned, shaking her head at Francie's statement. Then her face lit up. "Hey—the ring, Carla. You haven't talked about it yet, but I've read about the meaning behind a Claddagh. Are you being proactive and sending Jared a sign?"

"Ring? Claddagh?" The voices of Alice and Francie tumbled over each other.

I told them the story of Mick, Jamie, and the mysterious Claddagh, while Mel snapped a picture of it with her cell and texted it to the girls.

Alice said, "Carla, why didn't you let us know about the ring before? That's so cool." Makes sense that she'd be all about a "magical" element to my theoretical romance with Jared.

"I was going to tell you about it eventually."

"I've been asking," Mel said. "And she wouldn't say a word." She popped a sliver of apple into her mouth, knowing I was cornered at last.

"All right, I should have told you all when I first got it. I still look at the Claddagh and wonder if I should have accepted the thing. Mick said wearing the ring might help me decide if there's a future with Jared, but honestly when I look at it, I feel like I'm not quite myself. You know I never wear rings." I fiddled with it, spinning it around. "Necklaces and earrings, yes, but rings bug me when I'm sewing, so I've never developed the habit."

Many times, I considered taking it off and storing it on the handmade ring holder Emily gave me when she had her little shop on the town square.

"Whatever it takes, Carla," Francie said. "Wear the ring, or don't wear the ring. Find a sign, or go with your gut. All four of us know you're head-over-heels for Jared Barnett. *Do something about it.*" She paused. "Or else cut him loose and get back to your single life. There is nothing wrong with remaining single, you know. What stinks is hanging in limbo."

I wondered if that last statement was partly a reflection of her current situation.

I cleared my throat. "Thanks for your input, girls. Let's talk about something else."

Alice jumped in. "Wait. Just to clarify: you'll continue to date Jared without anticipating a future with him?" Her voice was incredulous.

"You do love him, right?" asked Mel.

"Yes, even though I'm afraid to, because if I don't get that sign I'm almost convinced there's no way we'll be happy together."

"What kind of sign are you looking for, Carla?" Francie's tone was a mixture of envy and disbelief.

I finished my wine. "I'm not sure, but I assume I'll know it when I see it."

Nobody had a rebuttal for that, and we spent the rest of our time simply catching up.

When we had all signed off I ended the call and started cleaning up the snack stuff. "I wish I hadn't admitted I'm looking for a sign," I told Mel.

"We all understand what you're talking about. I agree, if you and Jared are meant to be together, something will happen to clarify that fact, in no uncertain terms. Does Jared know?"

"Know what?"

"Does he know you love him, but you're waiting for a little bit of magic before you're ready to commit?"

"It's early in our relationship to talk about commitment." I ignored her use of the L-word. "And Jared is way too sensible to understand the idea of a *sign.*"

"I guess he is mostly a concrete thinker. Maybe he's moving slowly because of the kids. But Katie and Miles like you a lot."

"As far as I know, yes. Katie and I have been friends from the first. Being related to Matthew makes me special in Miles's eyes. Those two boys are tight."

She nodded. "No kidding. Miles is at our house part of every weekend, or else Matthew is at their place. The boys love to roam around the tree farm together. Like we did, only while brandishing sticks as boys are wont to do." Her brows lifted. "If things progress the way you and I both know they should, when you and Jared get married, do you think they'll move in here?" She gestured around the room. "Or will you go to live with them in the house on Shelby Street? That would sure be a change after being on the farm your whole life."

"Except for college."

"Yes."

"And frequent travel"

"Well, yes."

"I don't know, Mel. You're really getting ahead of things. There's no sign, no proposal, no marriage. So there's no need to decide a housing issue that doesn't exist."

"Trust me, when it does become an issue, it may be a challenge to decide. Jim and I had a heck of a time hashing it out."

"Yeah, I remember. The whole town probably remembers."

She laughed. "Maybe so. What chaos—but looking back, I wouldn't change a minute of it. I hope you get your own wedding memories, Carla. Assuming that's what you want."

"I just want to figure out what's next. In all my life I've never felt so unsettled."

Mel pulled me into a gentle hug. "Somehow everything will come together, honey. You just have to keep doing the right things, and trust."

What Mel and everyone else didn't know is that

long ago I had *not* done the right thing. That fact was in the forefront of my mind a lot these days, and part of me believed it might keep me from having a happily-ever-after. Or even deserving one.

Chapter Six

JARED STEPPED THROUGH the drapes into my workroom and I screamed.

"Now, that's some greeting. Does everybody get a scream, or just us special folks?" Laughing, he walked over to where I sat at one of my sewing machines, and kissed me.

My heart was racing from his unexpected appearance, and the kiss was over too soon. "I didn't hear you come in. Did the bell ring?"

"Yes, as always." He peered down at me, concerned. "Are you okay, Carla? You've been distracted lately."

"Sure. Yes, I'm fine. I was just focused on this..." I looked at the sewing machine. The fabric I should have been stitching was pooled in my lap, not on the bed of the machine at all. Evidently I'd gotten lost in my thoughts. Again. I looked at the Claddagh, which in spite of my insecurities, was still set to *taken*.

Jared followed my gaze. "Right. You're definitely focused on *something*. Would it help to talk about it?"

I shook my head, smiling up at him. "No reason to bother you with my issues."

He pulled a chair over, and took my hands in his. The Claddagh nudged the flesh of the fingers next to it.

"It's not a bother if I want to help, you know."

I laced my fingers with his. "I'll keep that in mind. Thank you, Jared."

Excitement transformed his face. "On the other hand, I have no qualms about coming here to blurt out exactly what's on my mind."

"Excellent. I'm ready to hear good news."

He released my hands and stood, too keyed up

to remain seated. "As we say in the land development biz, it's an idea with potential." He pulled a notebook from his shirt pocket. Jared is never without a small notebook and pen.

"There's an app for that, you know."

He chuckled as he flipped pages. "So you keep telling me. I just came from Exchange Club."

"Ah. That's why you're here so early." Exchange Club, a service group, meets each month at Chez Gwendolyn, the restaurant next door to my shop, for breakfast and an informational program.

"No leftovers for poor Carla sweating away at..." I glanced again at the neglected fabric in my lap. "Okay, skip that part. What happened at the meeting?"

"Mostly the usual. Great food, interesting program. Today's was about the upgrade planned for sidewalks around the square, to bring them up to ADA standards."

I stifled a yawn. Last night I hadn't slept well. Again.

Smiling, he shook the pen at me. "Wake up. I'm getting to the part you'll want to hear about. One of the guys—actually a couple of them who were sitting near me—mentioned that the city's economic development director is retiring."

"Oh, right. I did hear about that. His wife ordered a dress for his retirement party." I needed to get on that project too; I barely had time to complete it. "And?"

"And, these two guys at breakfast think I'd be a good fit for the position."

"Really?"

He crossed his arms over his chest, as if my single word had wounded him. "Yes, really. I do have a background and certain skills that might prove useful in helping attract business to Serendipity."

Oops. "Well of course you have fabulous skills, and whatever you don't know about the position, you'd be sure to learn quickly. So, what's-his-name is going to hang around a while and train whoever gets the job?"

"I don't know. I'd guess he will be willing to lend a hand. There's a great admin assistant in the office. I'm told she knows everything about the processes and contacts."

"I'll bet she does. Why don't they hire her to be the director then?"

He frowned. "They asked her to submit an application and she turned them down flat, not wanting the extra headaches. So you don't think I'd be any good as economic development director." It was a statement, not a question.

I had really stuck my foot in my mouth, hadn't I? "Jared, you can do whatever you put your mind to. I just—didn't realize you wanted to change careers. You've taken me by surprise."

He dropped the notebook and pen into a pocket. "Is it a surprise that I'd like to spend more time near home and fewer hours traveling up and down the state?"

"Only because it's what I'm used to you doing. Working close to home would make your life simpler, wouldn't it?"

He sat down again, perching on the edge of the chair. "Much simpler. I spend too many hours on the road. As things are now, Katie has a lot of responsibility with Miles, and I don't like pushing so much onto her. She's only fourteen, and I want her to enjoy her own friends instead of feeling like a nanny to her brother."

His expression darkened, and I could guess his thoughts. *If only Patty were still alive.*

I twisted the Claddagh. "Sure, I can see what you mean. I—if there are times I could help take up the slack when you have to be late, all you have to do is call or text." I had no idea how I could manage that, but the words were already out.

He took my hand again, holding it lightly. "Your workdays are long too. Not to mention travel. Thanks, Carla, but right now I'm making it work. I've got a system that keeps our days manageable. This E.D. job just sounds like a godsend, but I know nothing's perfect."

He was right—I was so busy, I didn't have extra time to do anything. The dress in my lap had to be completed today in order for me to stay on target for the month's projects. That meant I would work on it however many hours were required.

"I wonder who else will apply for the position. I

can't think of anyone *local* who would be qualified."

"Anyone *else* local, you mean," Jared said. "The guys told me I'd have to overcome that kind of attitude, but I didn't think of hearing it from you. They told me anyone with a history in Serendipity would have the best chance at getting the job, no matter their qualifications. The good old boy network is alive and strong in our fair community, but it's not doing a whole lot to help the town grow, is it? Remember, Carla— Serendipity is my hometown now, too."

I was dumbfounded—at his quick show of anger, and by what I had said to trigger it.

Jared left without another word. Off and on throughout the day I thought of our conversation. Did I exhibit the dreaded attitude that a new person who moves into town is never entirely one of us?

Chapter Seven

IT WAS A beautiful night for a cookout, which is always a possibility but never a certainty, this time of year. Even though I wasn't in a social mood, and sitting at home listening to my favorite CDs sounded like the perfect evening, I had stopped at the grocery after work and snagged my usual outdoor eating event contribution—a tub of potato salad and a tub of creamy cole slaw. We were celebrating Melissa's birthday at the cabin where she, Jim and Matthew lived. She said she had invited some friends as well as the family. I had somehow managed to be early.

I deposited the salads on the side table and hugged the birthday girl. "Wow, you're older than me again. I love how this works."

Mel laughed and took my proffered gift bag, her eyes alight. "Something you made?"

I shook my head. "Something from Ireland. I know, I cheated. I hope to make gifts again, once work slows down."

"Ah. Do you expect it to slow down?"

I shook my head, exhausted from an eleven hour day at the shop. "Not soon. I have another trip right away, too. New York. What I really need is undisturbed time in my workroom."

Jim left his preparations at the grill and put an arm around my shoulders. "Popularity must be horrible. Lawyers aren't afflicted with that problem."

I chuckled, and while Jim gave me a quick shoulder massage, the day's stress started to melt away. He stopped too soon and returned to his grill.

Matthew looked up at me, his eyes serious. "Aunt Carla, would you and Miles's dad please get married soon? Miles and me—" he caught his mother's glance—"Miles and *I* want him to be able to come to our family lunch on Sundays."

I had no words for him, uncertain even where I

stood with Jared right now. My mouth may have been hanging slack as I tried to form a response.

Jim turned from the grill again, and put a hand on his son's shoulder. "Matthew, you're always welcome to invite Miles for Sunday lunch. But I must tell you, the convenience of you and Miles, though important, isn't an ideal reason for your Aunt Carla to get married. Marriage is a very serious step." Jim shot me a look, one brow arched with meaning. Jim and Jared had gotten past their very negative start from the first time Jared visited Serendipity. At least I thought they were past it.

Matthew shifted his attention to his father, frowning in concentration. "I thought if you're grownups and you love each other and stuff, you get married. You and Mom did. And Uncle David and Aunt Emily." He looked again at me, the unasked question in his eyes. *Do you understand how this works, Aunt Carla?*

Melissa said nothing, but in the background she shrugged, grinning straight at me.

Thank goodness for Mom, who had stepped

onto the deck from the kitchen. "Now Matthew, let's not make Aunt Carla feel pressured." She leaned over and kissed the top of his head. "Grownups have to do things in their own time, honey."

"Seems awful slow, Grandma," he muttered.

She smiled. "That's because you're eight years old—everything takes a long time. The odd thing is, as you get older, life seems to pass much more quickly, just when you're wishing it would slow down." She gave Matthew a quick hug and another kiss, and went back to work organizing the food.

I was almost relaxed again when Jared's car came into view. I shot Mel a look.

"Yes, I invited them. Jared is my friend and a business contact. Plus I thought everybody would be glad to see Katie and Miles. It's been a while since we had them with us at a family event."

I wanted Jared and his kids to be part of our family, and I wanted to be part of theirs. But everything was so up in the air, inside my head. Yep, it was basically a disaster area up there. So many things seemed to point toward us remaining the way we were—separate.

Although he greeted everyone else in his usual relaxed way, Jared's smile for me was tentative.

Matthew and Miles excused themselves and tore off for the lake, promising to be back in time to eat.

Katie offered to help Mel in the kitchen. "I'm used to it. At home I cook a lot. Good thing Mom taught me."

Mel sent me a sweet-sad look over her shoulder as she and Katie went in the back door. To do what, I had no idea. I'm not a cook and don't care to become one. If not for excelling at everything about sewing, as well as design, color, and decorating, I would have failed home ec classes even in junior high.

Jared set a package of bratwurst onto the side table by Jim's grill. "Need any help, Jim?"

"No thanks, I'm good." Then Jim lowered his voice. "Cake?"

Jared nodded. "In the trunk, on a bed of ice in a huge cooler so it doesn't get sloppy. Just give me the signal when you want it to appear. I brought a flame thrower so we can easily get all the candles lit quickly."

Mom laughed and I couldn't help smiling. Mel and Jim are only a year older than I, and it's become frightening at recent birthday fetes how much like a forest fire our cakes are, once all the candles are lit.

"You think of everything, Jared," Mom said. "Carla, have you shown Jared the lake?"

"Mom, he and the kids lived on the farm that one Christmas season, remember?"

"But it's different this time of year." She inclined her head meaningfully toward Jared. "The two of you can check on those boys and be sure they're not getting into mischief."

None of us expected Miles and Matthew to get into mischief, unless you count fishing or stone-skipping.

Jared smiled at Mom. "It has been a while since I visited the lake." He held out a hand toward me. "Carla?"

Chapter Eight

WE WALKED IN silence, side by side. When we were out of hearing range of the cookout gang, I couldn't be quiet any longer.

"Jared, I'm sorry for the way I reacted the other day when you told me about the economic development director position. I don't have an excuse for my rudeness. The only reason I can offer is that I've been going through an emotional rough patch."

"Oh. Something to do with me?"

"It's not your fault."

He stopped, faced me and took both my hands. "That's not what I asked. If in any way I have caused you anguish, and if I can somehow remedy it, please tell me."

"It's not you directly. It's us, or the possibility of us. It seems everyone in town, particularly my family and closest friends, assume you and I are going to announce our engagement at any moment." I watched for his reaction, uncertain what I wanted it to be.

He smiled, slow and easy. "I'm still not used to the small town mentality. Everyone either knows their neighbor's business or is ready to create a feasible story." He shook his head, grinning. "So the people of Serendipity have decided you and I are at the edge of matrimony. And that is...a *bad* thing in your opinion?"

His jovial attitude calmed my nerves. "I'm not saying bad or good. I'm just telling you what the whispers are."

He took my hand. "I love you, Carla. You know that."

I nodded, tears forming in my eyes. "Yes, and I love you. I'm just not sure where we go from here."

Jared wrapped his strong arms around me. "We will figure it out, in our own time. You and I are in control of our relationship, not the rest of the town, or—whoever."

I wondered at his last word, but for a few minutes my world seemed perfect again, surrounded by Jared's arms and his love. Then he pulled back slightly, wiped some stray hairs out of my face, and kissed me. As usual, shock waves ran through me when our lips touched. I could only imagine, as indeed I occasionally did, what a further exploration would be like.

I don't know how long we stood there kissing, but eventually Miles and Matthew's voices were audible. Jared gave me a brief last kiss, and stepped back, keeping one of my hands in his. Holding his hand there on the farm where I had grown up felt good and right. A patch of evening sun made its way between the pine boughs and landed in the little glade where we had stopped.

And then the moment changed entirely, as the boys popped into view from the lake, the legs of their jeans soaked to the knees.

Jared and I chided them for having waded in the lake. Both boys were excellent swimmers, and I completely related to their story of trying to catch a turtle. Hadn't Jim, David and I done the same thing?

Possibly Francie too, but as the youngest she was sometimes left out of our adventures. Back in those days it was no big deal for us to roam the length and breadth of the farm at will. As long as we responded when Mom rang the dinner gong, we were golden.

I walked along holding Jared's hand, trying to focus on the story the boys were telling and Jared was reacting to. But my mind wasn't in the here and now; it was back in the days of my innocence and youth. So many wonderful memories were made on this farm, and some tough ones too.

A subtle breeze rustled the evergreen limbs and cooled my face, and I felt Dad's presence. How I wish I could talk to him about my relationship with Jared.

Mom had always been the organizer and supporter for us kids. But Dad—kind, fair, and pragmatic—was the parent we went to for advice. I needed a long in-depth talk with him. Then I would know where my life was headed, and if Jared was a small or large part of my future.

The breeze picked up. I slowed, and stopped. "You all go ahead. I'll catch up in a few. I just need a minute."

The boys seemed not to have heard, and went on chattering together headed toward the smell of barbequed meat. Jared let me pull my hand out of his, kissing my knuckles briefly before letting go.

"You okay, Carla?"

"Sure." I mustered a smile. "Don't let Jim eat everything in sight before I get there, okay?"

Jared nodded, looking a bit confused, but turned and walked away.

I went to the center of the group of Christmas trees. *Oh Dad, I miss you. I miss you every day, but right now I could really use some of your advice.*

Inhaling deeply, I relaxed in the unmistakable smell of home. Evergreens of all types surrounded me, their spicy fragrances mixed together in a way I've never experienced in any other place on earth. Yes, Dad was here with me, on the farm he'd loved so much, the one he and Mom had bought tract by tract and turned into the most popular Christmas tree farm in Southern Indiana.

Dad was here with me—with all of us—but he

wasn't going to step out fully formed from the far side of a plump blue spruce and wrap me in a bear hug. No, he wasn't here in body anymore—a fatal heart attack had seen to that. But he was still here in spirit.

In that moment a thought was emblazoned in my mind: I had to make peace with the history that was holding me back. Only then would I be ready for my future.

Tears rolled down my face. *I don't know how to make that peace, Dad.*

But the breeze was gone, and I didn't sense him anymore. In a few minutes I took a deep breath, wiped away the signs of tears as well as I could, and went to join the others.

Chapter Nine

WHEN KATIE CAME into the shop after school, she looked desperate in a way only junior high age girls can.

"Carla, I need help." She dropped into a chair at the consultation table, her long blond hair swirling briefly until it settled around her shoulders. "My dad is being impossible."

I didn't want to get between father and daughter, did I?

"Oh? What's up?"

She huffed out a dramatic sigh and crossed her arms over her chest. "The fall dance at school is coming up, and he won't let me buy a new dress."

Eighth grade dance. That made me feel old, as

there was no such thing back in my day. "He won't let you go to the dance? Or he said *yes* to the dance, but *no* to a new dress?"

"He finally said I can go because I told him the names of the girls I'll be hanging out with, and he knows some of their parents. I mean, he is *so* over-protective. But the dress—oh Carla, it's too awful." She had turned her head, but her eyes looked misty.

"Wait. I'm not following."

Katie still avoided making eye contact, but wrung her hands in her lap. "Grandma Peabody bought me a dress I can't wear. I didn't ask her to buy it, but I told her about the dance, and that I didn't have anything nice except what I'd outgrown and needed to get rid of. Last time we were at their house, she gave it to me. Dad said money is tight for us right now, and since Grandma gave me something new, I need to be grateful instead of complaining."

In my experience Katie is not a complainer, so there had to be more going on. "What's the problem with it? Is there something we can do to alter the dress?"

She shook her head, her eyes meeting mine at last. Looking near tears, Katie slid her cell out of her tiny handbag.

"I took a picture of it on a hanger in my room." She passed the phone to me and I recognized the problem.

"It's nice, Katie. Looks expensive."

She nodded. "Probably, knowing Grandma."

I cleared my throat. "Of course, the color—" The dress was a terrible choice for Katie's coloring. I realized not everyone understood such things, but was surprised at the dress Mrs. Peabody had bought. Situations like this are a fact of life for someone like Katie, who has a great eye for color as well as design.

Katie took the phone back. "I know Grandma Peabody was trying to be nice, and she thought it would be a fun surprise for me. But Carla, I *won't* wear that dress, ever." She looked away again. "Can you help me?" Her voice had dropped to a whisper.

Concerned about what she wasn't telling me, I touched her arm. "Honey, is something else wrong? Something besides the dress?"

She wiped at a tear. "I know it isn't your problem. I want to go to the dance, but unless I can wear something else, I'll stay home instead."

My mind was already working on possibilities. "If your dad doesn't want to spend money, how about I make one for you?" Not that I had any extra time in my schedule between now and—"When is the dance?"

"Three weeks."

"Oh my."

I understand the desire to have that one dress that makes you feel pretty. That's why *Creations* caters not just to the rich and famous who happily pay huge sums for their one-of-a-kind clothing, but also, when my schedule permits, to local women in search of a Cinderella memory. That included Mel's wedding gown, and the brocade skirt suit for the wife of the current Economic Development director.

"I'm pretty sure Dad would be mad about me getting another new dress. He would call it wasteful. He's on this reduce, reuse, and recycle kick."

"Ah. Those are all good."

She nodded solemnly. "I know. But this doesn't

fall into that category. Lately he's been hard to communicate with. He drives all over the place for work, and when he gets home he's always on the computer or at the library doing research. Can you talk to him, Carla? Make him understand this dance could be a turning point for me? When we first moved to Serendipity he constantly asked us if we were making friends at school, settling in, feeling comfortable. This dance is a big deal, but I know he thinks it's dumb."

If Jared didn't want to spend money on a dress, I would have to make the magic happen without an outlay of cash. An idea was forming. "You know what my customers sometimes call me?"

Nodding, Katie sat up straighter. "Fairy godmother. Because you make their dreams come true."

She jumped up and hugged me tight. "Oh, Carla, you're awesome. I knew I could count on you!"

My breath caught, standing there hugging the teenager who had stolen a piece of my heart. As Mel enjoyed pointing out, I had fallen in love with Jared the first time I met him. But I had also fallen for Katie, the twelve year old who walked through my shop entranced by the beautiful clothes, while it was obvious her grief for her mother was still strong. Miles, at age six, was miserable then too, so somber for a little guy. I'd known better than to act on my first inclination: to sweep him into a hug and tell him everything would be okay.

Katie stepped back, her smile brilliant. "What do we do first?"

I pictured my jammed-up work production calendar. "You look for some ideas and bring them to me, okay? That will help me with a design. I'll talk to your dad one on one about the dress from your grandmother. I don't want to go behind his back."

Katie retrieved her tiny handbag from the back of the chair she had vacated. "That's cool. You'll make it work out for everybody. Just like you always do."

She was gone then, and the bell over my door was still jingling when she disappeared down the sidewalk.

I looked around the shop to make sure everything was customer-ready as usual, and went through the drapes to the workroom where I spend so much of my life.

Make it work out for everybody, just like I always do. Right. No problem. The bell rang again and I chuckled as I did an about-face. *Now what? I should maybe round up some mice to serve as horses for the coach?*

But it was my sister-in-law, Emily. Though she's generally upbeat, at this moment she looked so happy, she positively glowed.

"Guess what!" She was nearly bouncing in place.

My heart skipped a beat when I recognized the answer on her face. "Oh my goodness. Emily—you're pregnant?"

She nodded and we flew into a hug.

"Oh honey, that's wonderful. I love happy news! When did you find out?"

"I did a home test last weekend when David was home, but I just came from the doctor. I can't call David right now because he's in meetings. And I don't want to tell him in a text." She rolled her eyes. "I want to tell my parents when David is home this weekend.

So I'm trying to keep this quiet, but can't." She hugged me again. "Carla, I immediately thought of you. Of all the people I know, you're the one who has it all together, all the time. So I decided to come over here and see if you can go to dinner with me for a quiet celebration."

"Wait a minute. Can we go back to how I *have it all together, all the time*? 'Cause let me tell you, that's not what it looks like from where I stand."

Emily laughed. "That's because you're such a perfectionist. You don't hold the rest of us to standards nearly as high as the ones you expect of yourself."

I worked on that for a moment. "Is that right?"

"Yes. So you're this perfect artisan, perfect family member, perfect friend, and perfect businesswoman."

I sounded quite impressive, but I knew better. "I don't cook, you know."

"Well, thank God for that, because if you could do everything well, I'd have to hate you."

"Ah. It's all good then."

"Yes it is. And this baby of mine is hungry, so

like I said, do you have time for dinner?"

Chapter Ten

WE HAD A delicious, fun, and I assume, baby-satisfying meal at Chez Gwen. A few days later the weekend rolled around, and David and Emily's happy news was broadcast—first to family and close friends. It wouldn't take long for the gossip tree of Serendipity to get hold of the information.

There was no other topic of conversation at Mom's house when the family got together for Sunday lunch. Matthew's take on the news was unique. "A cousin, *finally*. But a baby one. Watch it turn out to be a girl." He had said it softly, and I think mostly for my benefit, as he left the living room with Mom's faithful dog, Daisy, to go out in the yard and play.

Melissa was standing next to me, and inclined

her head toward the door. "Sit on the porch with me?"

Though I knew she was going to interrogate me again, I figured I'd just as well get it over with. We sat on the porch swing that had been there all my life, moving slowly at first, getting the cadence right and relaxing with the springs' gentle squeak in the background. Then Mel shifted a little toward me, raising one knee onto the swing while doing her part on propulsion with the other foot.

"How are you doing, Carla? You look tired."

Certainly not the conversation starter I had expected. Melissa is usually straight to the point. "I'm okay. Busy at the shop, and not exactly looking forward to the trip this week."

"What's the problem with the trip?"

I shrugged, staring across the porch and out toward the hills of Christmas trees. "Not a problem. My client pays well for the clothes, and who can quibble at free round-trip airline tickets to New York and a hotel suite while I'm there? Yeah, forget what I said."

Melissa laughed. "You know me better than that. You'd just as well come clean."

"Really, Mel, it's all good. I probably need to get away. A busy schedule with the client, but overall, this trip probably came up at the perfect time."

"Perfect because you don't want to deal with some local...issues?"

"Trust me, this is not the moment to lecture or prod me about Jared. He has a lot on his mind, and my plate is so full it's spilling out on all sides. It may sound backward to you, but I need some time away from the shop to figure out how I can possibly complete all the projects I have lined up. I love being busy, but right now I feel pulled in too many directions."

"Anything I can help with, Carla?"

I shook my head, looked down at the Claddagh. "Nope. I'll dig my way out of this somehow."

In spite of so many scheduled projects clamoring for attention, I needed to make Katie's dress a priority. She had brought me some pictures, and told me what she liked about the styles she had chosen. I could visualize the finished project, but wasn't sure how to find the time.

****

The night after Katie came to see me, Jared and I had a date. For some reason, at my age I cringe at the word *date*, but I don't know another one to use. This evening Katie and Miles both had 4-H meetings, so Jared and I typically have dinner together. In order to be able to speak to him privately about the middle school dance, I had made dinner. And when I say *made dinner* I mean, I put a frozen lasagna in the oven and opened a bag of salad, cut up a tomato and mixed it up.

We took our plates and wineglasses out onto the patio. The temperature was almost too cool, but I was wearing the wool sweater I had bought myself in Dublin on a previous trip.

Jared raised his glass. "Here's to my favorite Italian chef."

I clinked mine to his. "Aw shucks, Jared. You shouldn't make such a big deal of my ability to use packaged meals. But thanks anyway. Dig in."

He winked and picked up his fork, started working through the lasagna. "Nobody does it better than you, Carla."

After hesitating, watching him eat, I took a

steadying breath while setting my glass onto the table. "I need to talk to you about something serious."

He set down his fork. "Okay. Fire away."

"Katie came to see me. She really wants a new dress for the school dance."

He laughed, but without humor. "I realize that. I told her she could go to the dance. Patty's mom gave her a dress that's fine. It fits."

"She mentioned the dress from her grandmother. I'm not questioning your decision, but I really think it would be good if you reconsidered. Let me help Katie with this, okay? She's decent with a sewing machine, and if I make a pattern that's not too complicated maybe she could do most of the work herself. I haven't asked her about sewing class at school, but I know she was looking forward to it."

"There is no sewing class."

"What?"

"No sewing class. From what I heard at the PTA meeting, in order to get the kids up to speed on state standards, that's one of the classes that had to be cut."

"Home ec? But cooking and sewing are skills

everyone can use."

Jared smiled. "Some of us do pretty well without learning to cook, Carla."

I waved his comment away. "Packaged meals are expensive and not always the healthy choice. I'm not trying to be anybody's example on how to eat right. Cooking and sewing are important."

He shrugged. "I agree, but nevertheless they're gone."

"Well, what happened to Irene Glass, the home ec teacher?" Mrs. Glass would have a special place in Heaven, I was certain, due to her endless patience with my attempts to cook. She was my hero forever, because she taught me to sew. At that time she was a brand-new teacher.

"Early retirement, I guess," Jared said. "It happens."

"Ugh. That makes me sick. Well, Katie can use one of the machines at the shop." I made a mental note to re-launch the sewing class I used to host in January and February. Last year I was too busy to do it, but with this new development it was all the more important.

Had Katie told me about the class being canceled? She had been in school for a month now, and I had seen her several times in between my work and travel schedule. Maybe she hadn't wanted to bother me about it, but I wish she had.

Jared ran a hand through his hair. "I'm trying to teach my kids to be happy with what they have, instead of always being on the lookout for the newest, coolest item to add to their already overstuffed closets. Katie doesn't *need* a new dress, Carla."

"Actually, I think she does, and not to have the newest or coolest. I'm just trying to help, you know."

He briefly squeezed my hand. The Claddagh bit into my fingers. "I know. But I'm trying to help the kids learn gratitude. Do you hear what I'm saying?"

I nodded, unable to counter his point with anything he would relate to. The color of the dress was a non-issue to him. It existed, and it fit his daughter. In Jared's mind, that should be enough.

"Yes, I hear you. I'll definitely keep that in mind."

I knew Jared well enough to realize he would

stand firm on this. If I simply bought the material, created the dress and presented it to Katie, Jared would see it as undermining his authority. Whether or not he and I had a future together, I cared deeply for all the Barnett family, and wouldn't intentionally cause a rift.

Cue the Fairy Godmother.

Chapter Eleven

THE NEW YORK trip was a quick one, just a day meeting with a client, and another day in the fashion district for fun. I usually find the fashion district exhilarating, but on this trip everything was different. Each blond girl I saw in the city reminded me of Katie, every dark handsome man reminded me of Jared. So many families of four walked along the streets together, dined in the restaurants, checked in at my hotel, appearing happy and well-adjusted. Why couldn't our situation be that way—*normal*?

I was relieved to return to Serendipity where there was only one Jared, one Katie, and one Miles. And one me—the woman who others felt had it all together, but who was actually a big mess inside.

When I had dumped my suitcase in the bedroom and changed into jeans and a sweatshirt, I called Mom. As I'd hoped, she invited me up. I told her the highlights of my trip as we ate leftover vegetable soup.

When we had finished, she immediately hopped up and started clearing dishes. "Honey, I've got cookies to bake. Talk to me some more while I work?"

Of course there was no question of me helping with the cookies. We both knew that would be a bad idea. This evening's baking would be frozen until it was needed for the front counter of the Christmas shop, which would open on Thanksgiving evening. Daisy lay in a basket in the corner, knowing although many scraps came her way, Mom was strict about keeping chocolate out of the dog's diet.

We chatted about Mom's book club, new items she ordered for the shop, and the interesting guests at the B&B.

When the last batch was done and cooling on a countertop rack, Mom folded her tea towel precisely and faced me. "Carla, if there's something on your mind... No, let me start over. I *know* there's something on your mind, but for some reason you're not telling me. I'm not delicate, sweetheart. I've been back to one hundred percent for quite some time now."

"I know, Mom." We had all worried about, and hovered over her, after Dad died. The two had been nearly inseparable, and the first holiday season on the Standish family Christmas tree farm was especially rough for everyone. Francie had spent several months living with Mom and just being there whenever needed. Sometimes I wondered how that had affected my sister's marriage.

Mom worked so hard, and always had, to keep our family going. I should be helping with her load, not adding to it. I'd had a sense of Dad telling me to make peace with my history, but I couldn't stand to see the disappointment on her face, so I kept my problem to myself.

But I had another problem she might be interested in. "Mom, maybe you can help me with this situation I've wedged myself into, between Jared and Katie." I told her about the dance and the dress.

"Yes, that's awkward, Carla." She paced the

kitchen, humming quietly, and carrying the tea towel. A few minutes later she turned toward me. "I respect what Jared is teaching his children, and maybe this is a way to honor that, while also helping Katie create something unique."

I recognized the spark in Mom's eye. "I like it so far even though I have no idea what you're talking about."

"You said Katie has old party dresses that are too small." Mom held up her tea towel which was trimmed with quilt squares. "If she has a style she likes, and could use fabric from those dresses to create it, she would be using her artistic talent by incorporating design and color in a unique way."

Possibilities flashed into my mind. "I love it! One of the photos she brought me was a simple slip dress. It would be easy to make one of those out of several fabrics, and maybe top it with a teeny shrug of one color." I hugged her. "Mom, this is perfect. The only problem is getting the time to work on it."

Mom's smile widened. "I hear Irene Glass is out of a job."

It didn't take long to call my old home ec teacher and set up a meeting with her at my shop. She loved the project idea, and could set up in my workroom to help Katie with it. Irene and her husband live way out on Walnut Ridge Road, so Katie wouldn't be able to go to Irene's home.

I gave Mom a hug and kiss as I left. "Once again, you've saved my bacon. You're really good at this motherhood thing."

She stood in the front doorway of her house for a while, watching me as I walked through the gathering dusk toward my own home. Tonight was clear and crisp. We four kids had been raised in the big, white frame house in the center of the farm. In some ways, it's still the center of our lives.

In addition to my house, Jim and Melissa's, and David and Emily's, tiny cabins have been sprinkled throughout the farm. That was Mel's idea, the first year we were without Dad, and uncertain whether it was feasible to keep the Christmas tree farm going since we would have to hire workers to do much of what Dad had always taken care of. The tiny cabins are a year-round bed and breakfast business, run by Mom and Emily. Back before the tiny cabins, Jared Barnett was known to all of us simply as the land developer from Indianapolis who was trying to push Mom into selling the farm.

Ugly days. But now we all understand that he wasn't really himself back then. His wife was dying, and he and his kids were doing what they could for the woman they loved, while trying to imagine how they would get along without her.

Shadows of pain and loss still crossed their faces at times expected and unanticipated. A holiday, a piece of music, a book she loved. And, like the old gentlemen in Dublin said, when photos are shared. At those moments, I felt like an outsider. Who was I to be in a romantic relationship with Patty's husband? Who was I to be hugging her son after a soccer game, or congratulating her daughter at a school art show?

I never met Patty, and only heard about her after she died. Who was I to want her family to be mine?

Maybe that would never happen, and I would only be the woman who tried, in her haphazard manner, to help them feel comfortable in Serendipity. Maybe Katie would remember me as the nice lady who helped her learn to sew.

Could I be satisfied with fulfilling those roles instead?

Chapter Twelve

IN THE CHECKOUT at the grocery I stepped into the wrong line, but this time it wasn't wrong because the queue moved slowly. This time I regretted my choice because of the conversation taking place.

"He isn't even *from* here," the woman ahead of me said to the checkout girl. "How does that Barnett guy have the gall to apply for a big paying job that somebody from Serendipity ought to get? A lot of our local people don't even *have* jobs."

The checkout girl nodded, sliding items through the scanner down to the bag boy. "I heard he has an inside track. That no matter who else applies, Barnett's going to get it." She shrugged. "Politics."

The customer made a *tsk*-ing sound. "I hadn't

heard that. But I'm not surprised. He sure managed to get cozy with all the right people in a short time. Power-hungry is what he is. Already has plenty of money anyway. Just look at that big house he bought. I heard he paid cash for it."

"Really? Wow. He seems nice enough when he comes through my line, but you can't always tell by that."

"Not at all. A friend told me his teenage daughter is wild. We sure don't need that kind of people moving into Serendipity. And then there's the boy. He's young yet, but watch out in a couple of years. He has a ridiculous name...can't think what it is just now."

I lost the fight to try to stay quiet, let the woman's nastiness expend itself, and move on.

"So is there a large pool of applicants for the position?" I asked.

The customer swiveled around and glared at me. "How should I know?"

I slid a plastic divider between her grocery order and mine. "Maybe the article in this week's paper will have actual *facts*. I'm sure that's what you're looking for, as opposed to gossip invented by people with nothing better to do." I stacked my frozen dinners onto the conveyor. "Seems to me Jared Barnett is very qualified for leadership in that position."

She looked me up and down. "Oh yeah. You're *seeing* him, aren't you?" Her enunciation of *seeing* made it sound vulgar.

I shrugged. "Seeing him or not, I can't imagine anyone who would do a better job as economic development director. Did you apply?"

"Ha! Of course not. It isn't my kind of job. I know people who would do great at that though."

"Well let's hope those friends of yours sent resumes, and applied for the job. My understanding is that a committee oversees all that."

She smirked. "Hmm. And are you on the committee?"

I slammed my gallon of milk onto the belt. "Sadly, no." I bared my teeth in what probably failed to look like a smile. The bag boy, having appeared uncomfortable during the mini stand-off with Ms.

Know-it-all, took off toward the parking lot with her cart of groceries. The mean-spirited woman, whom I recognized but didn't know personally, had to hurry to catch up with him.

A few minutes later, I allowed myself to seethe as I not-so-gently set my groceries into the trunk of my Mustang. Jared had applied for the job. Had he met with the committee already too? He hadn't shared more about the possibility since his first inclination of *maybe* applying.

That hurt. Either we were a couple, or we were not. It didn't bode well if he hadn't kept me up to date about a life-changing event like having a job in town instead of traveling all over the state. Hurt and angry, I was tempted to drive from the grocery straight to his house and confront him about it. But the kids would likely be there, and I didn't want to blow up in front of them. It was Tuesday night, an evening that was generally free of after-school running, so the three of them would be home having dinner together, doing homework, and maybe playing a game or watching a video in the big, comfortable living room. Meanwhile I had worked another long day to complete sketches I would present to a customer tomorrow during an online chat.

It was important that I kept projects coming in, and completed them on time. Especially since I didn't have anyone to support me if I failed. I had been on my own since reaching adulthood, and with this snub from Jared, it seemed likely I would remain that way. I would be fine with or without joining my life to Jared's. I just wanted to know where I stood, and to be sure the kids weren't hurt by our on again-off again relationship.

At the stop light waiting to turn onto Main Street from the grocery parking lot, I glanced down at my right hand. The Claddagh was registering *looking/available*.

Not really looking, but rather, weary from years of dating. How many wrong guys had I fallen into relationships with over the years? The light changed to green and I turned left, toward either Jared's house or the tree farm. I drove halfway around the square, past my shop on the right and the courthouse in the center of the green space. When I reached the intersection with

State Road 56, I wasn't certain whether to turn right toward home or not. Almost of its own volition, the Mustang shot ahead when the light turned green—north on Main, made the turn on Homer and in a moment's time pulled into the short drive next to Jared's house. I sat there trying to calm my breathing, spinning the Claddagh on my finger.

Chapter Thirteen

JARED OPENED THE door almost immediately. His face broke into a wide grin and he enveloped me in a hug. "Hey, Carla. I thought I heard your car." He pulled back and looked down at me. Evidently registering my state of mind, he pecked my cheek instead of going for a full-on kiss. "Okay. Tell me what's wrong."

"Jared, according to the Gossip Tree, you applied for the economic development job."

"Right. I told you about that, remember?"

"You said someone suggested it to you. That was all. You never mentioned it again."

"I didn't get the idea you were interested in hearing about it. In fact, I felt like you didn't think I was a good candidate, due to being an interloper in the community."

"Interloper. I didn't say that." *Did I?*

"Whatever. Due to not being born in town, you consider me unqualified. But I disagree, and so have several people whose opinions I value. So I dusted off my resume and applied. Why are you angry?"

"Like I said, because you didn't talk to me about it."

"Beyond being shot down at the outset, I figured we were both better off if I followed my instincts. The committee makes the final decision anyway, so the matter is out of our hands at this juncture." He cocked his head, looking deep into my eyes. "You'll be disappointed if I get the job?"

"No, of course not. It would be wonderful if you could work here in town. Much nicer for the kids."

He frowned. "For the kids," he repeated.

"They're your focus after all."

"My first focus. Not my only one." He took my hand but I pulled out of his grasp and stepped back.

"Then why didn't you tell me you had applied, Jared? Couples discuss life changes like this. Even *potential* life changes."

His chin dropped. "I see what you mean. Maybe I should have talked to you more about it. I thought you might be negative again, and I didn't want to hear it. I've become accustomed to keeping my own counsel since..."

Since Patty died.

He continued, "I might point out that you don't consult me when planning trips to visit your customers. You just announce that you're leaving the next day for Dublin, New York, or Timbuktu. I smile and nod, offer a ride to or from the airport if I can work it into the schedule I've already got planned."

"That's the way I've always done it, Jared. I'm a one-woman business."

He nodded. "Try to see what's going on here. We're both doing our own thing, making decisions that affect each other without checking in. This isn't just about me and the E.D. job, or about you leaving town with little—and sometimes *no* notice."

My chest hurt and I realized I'd been holding my breath.

"What is it about then?" I asked.

"It's about deciding whether we want to keep functioning as we are, or trying a different model."

"I'm not sure how good I'd be at checking in ahead of time."

Jared shoved his hands into his pockets. "I guess it depends on what your goals are, doesn't it?"

****

By the time I pulled into my garage, I had almost managed to calm down. I carried my groceries into the kitchen and stacked my dinners in the freezer, checked the milk jug for leaks before sliding it onto the fridge shelf. I poured a glass of wine and slid open a patio door, carefully set the glass onto the table and stood with eyes closed, trying to feel the sense of peace the Christmas tree farm affords me. The variety of pine scents floated around me, and I silently named each type of tree they represented.

Was I going to end my relationship with Jared? Is that what I wanted to do? In spite of going behind my back about the job, he had been genuinely surprised that

I was upset about it. He made a good point about my own schedule, but I had been running my life and business this way for almost twenty years. Could I become that woman who checks with her guy before she makes a client appointment?

Did I even want to become that woman? I barely had time to do my work and make the travel arrangements, let alone adding in a step of asking permission from Jared.

A man who thought I should change the way I operated, a somewhat dramatic teenage girl wanting a dress her dad forbade, and the unknowns of relating to an elementary age boy—all of them still missing the wife and mother who had died so young. Why complicate my life by staying involved?

My status quo was ideal: successful business, cozy house, fabulous friends, and a family I loved—and with Jim's and David's marriages the family was growing. My life was perfect just the way it was.

Jared Barnett was a nice guy, and I had enjoyed spending time with him and his kids. They were a family without Patty, just as the Standishes were still a family without Dad. Important people move in and out of our lives, but losing them physically isn't the end. Jared was a great father, and he would figure out the right way to deal with whatever Miles and Katie ran up against. That's the way great parents are. They don't need assistance from the outside, or advice from people who may mean well but really don't have a clue how to raise kids.

I'd been fooling myself to ever believe the Barnett family needed me. What an overblown ego! Had I tried to push away their memories of Patty, to put myself in her place? Not intentionally, but surely every time I engaged Katie in girl talk around the shop, or tempted Miles with an ice cream cone, it was an effort to get my foot in the door of their family circle, so to speak.

It was a good thing I realized before the relationship went on any longer. From here on out, I would be as nice as ever to them, but no closer personally than any other Serendipity citizen. Let the Barnetts go on with their lives, and I would go on with mine. I had been happy enough before meeting the family and getting caught up in their drama. Much happier, in fact.

I slid the patio door shut, nuked a frozen dinner, and poured another glass of wine. Before consuming my meal while standing at the kitchen counter, I removed the Claddagh ring. As much as I had wanted to believe something special would happen because of it, I didn't believe it anymore. Remembering the funky turquoise ring holder Emily had given me when she had her little shop, I slid the ring onto it. I took a step back, observing how pretty it looked on the little open-shelved stand in the living room.

The windows were shut tight, and it made absolutely no sense that I thought I heard the wind whispering to me about making peace with the past.

Chapter Fourteen

MELISSA STARTED VERBALLY working me over at lunch time as soon as she dropped her bag onto the table in the workroom.

"Carla. Get hold of yourself, woman. You are sabotaging your relationship with Jared for what reason?"

"He and I aren't meant to be together. Can we talk about something else?"

"Of course you're meant to be together. Any fool can see that. And yes we can talk about something else as soon as you tell me you're going to give it another try with him."

"You asked my reason and I gave you one. We don't belong together. I could just ask you to leave, you know."

"Okay. I'll reword my request. Give me a *good* reason. And by the way, although you could ask me to leave, it wouldn't do you any good."

I unzipped my lunch bag, resigned to the fact that I was in for another bout of back and forth with Mel. "If Jared and I aren't meant to be together, that's the best reason ever. You and Alice and Francie keep pushing me toward him. That we dated in the first place was probably something you three worked together on, am I right? You shoved him toward me, nudged him to ask me out."

"Don't be ridiculous. The man fell in love with you the first time you met, that first day I walked around the square with them before taking them out to look at houses. I was a witness to the moment. So were Matthew, Miles and Katie, although I doubt any of them were aware of the sparks shooting between you and Jared. Katie was looking at dresses, and Miles and Matthew were talking trucks."

I watched her, looking for a sign she was fibbing. "Hmm. I always thought it was someone else's idea that he ask me out the first time."

"Not that I know of, unless Katie suggested it to her dad. Since she *worships* you." She shot me a look. "How does this breakup, if that's what you've done, affect your friendship with Katie? Are you kicking her to the curb too?"

"Mel! What a horrible thing to say. Of course Katie is always welcome to come by and work on projects, visit, whatever." I felt hollow. I would miss Katie more than she would miss me if her visits ceased.

"Doubtful she'll feel comfortable doing that, with you dumping her father."

"Well, I hope she will. I'll text her."

"For Katie's sake, I hope she'll continue to spend time with you. She needs a woman she can confide in, you know. Your mom was that person for me when I was Katie's age. My own mother couldn't have cared less."

I wondered about Katie's dress. I hadn't heard from her since the blowup Jared and I had at their front door.

Melissa put a hand on mine. "What's Jared

supposed to do, Carla? He's a single dad trying to raise his kids in a world that is more complicated every day. He was starting to rely on you, blend their lives with yours. Then you shut him down, tell him he's all wrong for the economic development director job. How could you, Mel? He's trying to find his place here, along with doing his best for the kids."

"He asked what I thought, and I told him. Might have been a little quick to judge..."

"Gee. Ya think? Jared can make a huge difference for Serendipity if he gets that job and things start to happen around here. Not a moment too soon either. I know you don't have to worry about the economic climate of the town since most of your income is from the rich and famous. But Carla, if our local economy continues in the direction it's been going, you're likely to see fewer and fewer orders from local people. I wouldn't be surprised if my wedding gown is your last, for Serendipity brides. Who's going to be able to afford one?"

I muttered, "I've been sort of considering getting out of the bridal business."

Mel laughed. "You can't kid me. Those bridal gowns are your favorite part of having a dress shop."

I sighed. "Guilty. And I do read the local paper, Mel. Not every issue, and not when I've been traveling, but I sort of keep up with community news. It's a little hard to miss the empty storefronts on the square, where thriving businesses were located not so long ago. In the last ten years two factories shut down and a lot of people started commuting to the Louisville area to work. I do realize that."

"The *lucky* ones are commuting, if you can refer to spending ten or more hours a week on the road as lucky. Some never found another job at all. Do you know the percentage of kids in the elementary, middle, and high schools who are eligible for free or reduced price lunch? It's staggering."

"I didn't realize. But we're not likely to bring in another industrial facility, are we? How can Serendipity grow when so many consumer goods are made overseas?"

"I don't know, Carla, and I think we need a savvy businessman with good contacts and the ability to encourage us to look at options the rest of us might never consider. I think we need someone who isn't *from here*. Heck, I got that treatment when I first came back to Serendipity after being gone. Talk about closed-minded! Our town really can't afford to maintain that attitude. It's going to kill us."

"Thanks for the lecture, Mel. I see what you mean, and you've given me loads to think about. Mom called and invited me for dinner tonight. Am I going to get a similar treatment there?"

Mel put her empty sandwich and chip boxes back into her bag and zipped it. "I have no idea. She and I aren't doing an intervention, although it's an idea I'll keep in mind for later, if it's still necessary. Maybe your mom just has leftovers she wants to share."

"Yeah, I doubt it. I got a vibe from her that she has something important to talk to me about. Yikes."

Chapter Fifteen

MOM HAD CALLED the shop and asked me to have dinner with her. Home-cooked food and not even on a Sunday? Of course I accepted. I didn't work as late as I had been recently, but locked the back door of my shop at a decent hour, carrying a box of work to do at home. As I walked to my car I pulled my hair back and braided it quickly, put the top down on my Mustang and took the countryside route home, via Market Street and past the county fairgrounds. I usually stick to the highway, but occasionally prefer the twists, turns, and hills of the backroads. Driving anywhere is fun in the Mustang, and I was really in need of cheering up. I felt dried up and dead inside, as if I had never enjoyed a day in my life. I also felt as if I'd been punched in the gut repeatedly, thanks to my dear friend Mel. I hoped Mom's invitation was without agenda.

Mom was buzzing around the kitchen, chatting about the current tiny cabin B&B customers and the arriving orders for Christmas shop inventory. "Carla honey, could you please get the bowl of fruit salad out of the fridge for me?"

I obeyed, amazed as always that Mom cooks often, even now Dad is gone. There were several neatly-labelled containers of leftovers lined up in her fridge, arranged in order of expiration date.

"Mom, do you serve leftovers to the B&B peeps at all?"

"Goodness, no. You know they wouldn't appreciate that. Fresh everything, every single morning."

"That's a lot of work."

"Yes. Anything worthwhile is worth working for. Wouldn't you agree, honey?"

Why didn't I think we were talking about leftovers anymore? Or the B&B?

"Yes, I suppose so." I searched for a not-about-me topic. "How's Emily? I haven't seen her in a few days."

"She's wonderful. Eventually, closer to her due date, I'll need to replace her. Get someone else to do most of the cleaning for the cabins. I do a little now, but Emily handles most of it. She and I are discussing some possibilities. Plenty of people need work around here, that's for sure."

"Right. Mel was talking about that earlier today."

She motioned me to a chair at the kitchen table, the cozy spot in the heart of her home where so many discussions have taken place through the years. When we were growing up, the dining room was used only on holidays, or if we had friends over and the whole group wouldn't fit around the kitchen table.

Now the dining room is used on Sunday afternoons for our family meal, and from late November through the end of the year, B&B customers have their breakfast there. The rest of the year, Mom and Emily serve breakfast in the Christmas shop building, re-arranged for that purpose.

I pulled out the chair that had been mine, back in the day when all of us kids lived at home. Mom sat at her old place too, which coincidentally was on the end next to me. Daisy staked out a spot between us, in case of dropped food.

"I think I know what's been bothering you lately, Carla. Last time you were here, I asked you, but we ended up talking about Katie."

"That project is going to work out. I heard from Irene late this afternoon. She's talked more to Katie, and they will be working at the shop." That had been a huge relief, though the fact that the word came from Irene and not Katie was a concern. "Katie seemed hesitant to cut up her old dresses, but Irene is bringing a gorgeous crazy quilt to show her. It's velvet, silk, satin—all sewn with a variety of stitches in bright colors. It's a stunning work of art. That will help Katie envision what she might do."

Mom nodded. "I'm glad to hear it. Sounds like a good thing for everyone involved. But what I want to talk to you about isn't Katie's problem, but something you have carried around as a problem for a long time."

"Sounds mysterious, or like I've been unbalanced for years."

Mom handed me the bowl of tossed salad. "I'm talking about the ring."

I dropped the salad tongs. They bounced off the table and landed on the floor. Daisy shuffled backward and seated herself again, uninterested in licking a pair of salad tongs.

I retrieved them from Mom's spotless floor and rinsed them at the sink, keeping my back to her as I asked, "Ring? What... What ring?"

I returned to my seat and Mom shook her head, that sad smile still present.

My face started to burn in embarrassment. "Grandma's? You know about that?"

"Of course I know, honey. Remember what I always told you children. I'm the mom. I know everything. That was bit of a stretch, of course."

I shook my head to clear it. "You know about the ring. Who told you?"

"You did, Carla. Without saying a word."

But I hadn't told her, or anyone else. "I was

afraid you would find out and be disappointed in me, or angry." My head dropped. "Both of which I deserve."

****

The day it happened, I was about five years old. Jim would have been six, and David, four. That would make Francie three years old the day we were hauled to a wedding in town. I don't remember who got married. I do recall that the bride's gown made me think of Cinderella. I think it was the first wedding I had attended. The boys and I were still in our dress-up clothes because Mom had taken our fussy baby sister indoors for a belated nap. Maybe she was also working on dinner. Dad had gone to check something out on the farm.

We kids were always close, and for the most part we got along. Here's why—we took turns choosing what we would play. Sometimes I was a bad guy, pretending to ride a mean black horse, being chased by my brothers who were the posse. Or we played Tarzan, and I was Jane, or a native. Jim was usually Tarzan, and David the bad safari guy who wanted to shoot him. We fit Francie in wherever we could, like being Cheetah following Tarzan around, flopping her arms and making chattering noises.

When it was my turn I usually chose to play Knights, because the boys liked going at each other with long sticks, and I could wear a beautiful costume of my own creation. Francie didn't get a turn to choose very often, until she was old enough to realize that she should. She'd squeal, "Let's play school!" or almost worse, "Let's play house!" The rest of us would groan, but have to follow through. This afternoon due to Francie's nap, there were just three of us, and it was my turn to choose the game.

"Let's play wedding."

The boys complained pitifully, but they knew if they didn't play my game, I wouldn't play theirs next time. (I was an excellent Wild West bad guy, and a passable Jane, instructing Francie's Cheetah and keeping her in line.)

I chose Jim to be the groom because he was taller. David could be the preacher and I of course would be the bride. I dashed into the house and borrowed a doily off the couch for my veil. Then I quietly went into Mom and Dad's room and took out the ring. Grandma Standish had shown it to me not long before she died.

"Carla, as the oldest girl, you will get this ring for your very own when you're ready. Your mother will keep it safe for you, but when it's time, you can have this ring when you find the man you want to marry. Your grandpa and I were married for many years, and were very happy. That's what I want for you, sweetheart."

The diamond wasn't large, but it caught the light like nothing I'd ever seen. I knew Grandma wouldn't mind if we played wedding with it. After all, it was mine and Mom was just holding it for me.

We did our little pretend wedding, Jim slid the ring onto my too-tiny finger. We didn't kiss of course— gack—but David pronounced us man and wife.

I don't know how it happened, despite replaying the ever-more-grainy mental videotape thousands of times over the years. Maybe we played another game, and I set the ring somewhere for safekeeping. When

Mom called us in to change and have dinner, the ring was nowhere to be found. I swore the boys to secrecy and as far as I know they never said anything. I haven't mentioned it to either of them in all these years. After all, it was no one's fault but my own. Grandma Standish had given me her happily-ever-after ring, and I had lost it.

As time passed, my little girl fear of getting into trouble for my actions evolved into something more. My future was tied up with that ring. Many times I gave the yard a going-over. There was no finding it, and no releasing myself from the need to do so.

****

Mom's smile was wistful. "I watched you children playing that day after the wedding. I didn't realize you had sneaked Grandma's ring out of our bedroom, but you were upset when I called you in to change and eat dinner. You cried yourself to sleep that night, but wouldn't tell me what had upset you. The boys seemed clueless that anything was wrong."

"Men. Even single-digit-age men."

She chuckled. "At some point I realized the ring was missing, and put that fact together with your tortured attitude. I gave you every opportunity to tell me the truth. I'm sure you don't recall, since you were so young at the time."

"I felt like a horrible person for losing the ring." *And to some extent I still do.*

"I wonder now if I should have confronted you with the facts, and punished you. Maybe then you'd have let the accident fade into the past. I forgot about it ages ago, but something you said the other day brought the incident back to me. Carla, have you punished yourself all these years about that ring?" She looked into my eyes, evidently finding the answer there.

Mom got up and walked behind me, put her arms around me and rested her chin on my head.

"Sweetheart, I'm here to tell you, it's time you stopped beating yourself up over a mistake made so long ago. My goodness, we all do things we regret."

"But Grandma Standish told me about the ring, and trusted me to grow up and use it."

Mom kissed my temple, then straightened and

stood behind me, smoothing my hair as she had done when I was a little girl.

"Carla, Grandma loved you. She would never have wanted you to torture yourself over a piece of metal and a stone. Love is so much more important than a ring, or any inanimate object. When you're in love and ready to marry a man, whether or not that man is Jared Barnett, a ring is part of the process because humans have created a tradition. Even those beautiful wedding gowns you design aren't *necessary* to happiness, are they?"

I shook my head, tears running down my cheeks. I had created a fabulous dress for Melissa, but her wedding turned out to be very different than planned. Different, yet perfect.

"Now eat your dinner before it gets cold. And think about what I've said."

I knew I would have a very hard time thinking of anything else.

I lay awake that night, thinking about what Mom had told me. She had forgiven me, and wanted me to forgive myself. On the night of Mel's birthday cookout, I'd had the sensation that Dad was telling me to let go of that bit of my history.

Mom's words seemed to flow along the walls of my darkened bedroom like advertisements on Times Square: *Carla, Grandma loved you. She would never have wanted you to torture yourself over a piece of metal and a stone. Love is so much more important than a ring, or any inanimate object.*

If I could put aside my long-ago error in judgment, I also needed to let go of the idea that I would get a bit of magic, as Mel and Alice had experienced. I had a strong feeling that the bit of magic I would have had, involved Grandma's ring. But I knew it wasn't just the mistake of losing the ring that stood between me and happiness with Jared. I had really botched things with him, and with Katie and Miles. I knew I wanted another chance, and that to get it, I would have to do something big. Something way outside my comfort zone.

Chapter Sixteen

I<small>F WHAT</small> J<small>ARED</small>, Katie, and Miles needed was a woman who cared enough to prepare their evening meals and create a homey atmosphere, I could become that woman. I wasn't stupid after all. How hard could it be to read a cookbook and prepare a nice meal for my family? I wanted them to be my family, and was ready to make efforts I had never been inclined to make in the past.

If they got wind of my new endeavor, my brothers would tease me mercilessly, so I couldn't borrow a cookbook from Mel or Emily. Mom might have a heart attack if her nontraditional daughter asked to borrow a cookbook. Plus, I didn't want to wade through the dozens of choices from Mom's cookbook library, which takes up a bookcase created by Dad just for that purpose in a corner of the kitchen.

Therefore, to avoid catching grief from anybody, I picked up a copy of *The Joy of Cooking* at a bookstore in Louisville on the way home from a client visit. I figured it must be a great cookbook because it was so big. Plus, I had heard of it, which is impressive in itself.

I sat at my kitchen bar and pored over the huge tome of cooking knowledge. *Seriously*. It went on forever, telling every possible bit of information about everything one could describe as food. Overwhelmed, I slammed the book shut, pulled my phone near, and started an online search for menus.

I settled on one that sounded impressive and yummy, while also having a local flair: Capriole goat cheese served with lavash for an appetizer, followed by a mixed green salad tossed with sunflower seeds, shredded carrots and tahini dressing. Then osso bucco served over polenta, and vanilla ice cream with shards of homemade peanut brittle sprinkled over the top for dessert.

The combination was different enough to be interesting, and my going to the effort would help demonstrate that I loved them all.

I found a sheet of notebook paper and wrote a grocery list. Good thing I'd chosen a full sheet too, because I needed every bit of the space.

The checkout clerk gave me some odd looks as she rang up all the ingredients. "Wow, Ms. Standish, this is different from what you usually buy." She held up the osso bucco and her eyebrows disappeared under her shaggy bangs. "Yeah. Really different. You having company?"

Pretending not to hear her question, I slid my credit card into the reader, shocked at the total. I never spend this much at the grocery. Of course I'd had to buy enough corn syrup and every other ingredient for the peanut brittle, to make several batches. Why don't stores have a special section for *I'm not sure I'll ever want to use this again, so I'll just have a teensy bit?*

But, I reminded myself, this was just my first outing as a cook. Once my kitchen was fully stocked— for the first time ever—I wouldn't have to buy basic supplies often.

I had called Jared and invited them to dinner as an apology for my blowup about the E.D. job. He was gracious, accepting without further comment on the rest of that evening's discussion.

They would be at my house for appetizers (how exciting to even plan to serve an appetizer) and dinner at six o'clock Saturday evening. I had chosen Saturday because I close the shop at noon, and I figured I would need a bit more time than the average cook. At least this first time, while I was learning. With a few more outings I should get up to speed.

Just shows you how little I knew about cooking. Hello! Homemade peanut brittle? I started with it first, so the stuff could be cooling while I created the rest of the spread. What a mess. Not just the peanut brittle, which hardened to the point I couldn't chip it out of the pan, but when I had finished that effort, most of the kitchen was a disaster. I set the peanut concrete on the dining table and cleaned all the surfaces in the kitchen before starting on the polenta. Why, oh why wasn't there some kind of a warning on this online site that promised *easy homemade meals*? At the very least there should have been a difficulty rating, preferably one that included a big red circle and a line across it, with polenta and peanut brittle in the center of the circle.

Lavash? Give me a break. Before hitting the grocery, I had read the recipe several times, and tried to imagine going through all those steps just in order to have homemade "cracker bread" instead of buying it. In order to keep from having a meltdown—I hoped—I had dropped the bucks and wimped out on the lavash. Plus obviously without having my own goat, I would not be making goat cheese. I felt these were excellent, reasonable decisions that would incidentally free me up to concentrate my efforts on the rest of the meal.

Results so far looked like at least the appetizers would be edible.

Osso bucco and polenta were double disasters to the kitchen, but at least the meat smelled good. When my guests arrived, my heart started to race.

Katie sniffed her way to the kitchen. "Hi, Carla. Dinner smells good." She smiled but her eyes warily scanned the disaster area.

"Hi, Katie. I hope it tastes good too. I might have gotten in over my head with my plans for tonight. At least there's an appetizer though. It's there on the dining table." I preceded her, scooped up the disastrous peanut brittle with a sheepish grin. "Not this. This was kind of an experiment." *Gone very, very wrong.*

Katie handed the always-hungry Miles a piece of lavash just as Jared hugged me and kissed the top of my head.

"Hey, you. What can I do to help?"

I didn't know the answer besides *suggest we go out for dinner*, but it didn't matter because Miles was spitting out the appetizer.

"Miles!" Jared's face turned red. "Clean that up."

Katie's grabbed a paper towel and helped her brother mop crunchy goat cheese off the hardwood floor. Jared was reaching into the basket of lavash.

"Dad, smell that cheese first," Miles said, shifting his gaze from Jared to me.

I had a taste a few minutes prior, and thought it was good. "What? Is there something wrong with it?"

Miles's look of disgust said it all. "What *is* it?"

"Goat cheese. Local stuff, really healthy."

Jared shook his head, chuckling, and spread a piece of lavash with cheese, popped it in his mouth. His brows rose in appreciation, and I poured him a glass of wine. Then I poured a big glass of water for Miles. He drank thirstily and with relief, standing some distance from any area that contained food. I poured wine for myself and had a gulp.

"Carla, it tastes great to me," Jared said. "I don't think the kids have experienced goat cheese before. It does have a unique flavor." He was smiling at me, but also managed to look a bit stern at the kids. "You should try it, at least a tiny bit of it. Once you know it's not like something you've had before, your taste buds will get the idea and maybe enjoy it."

Katie and Miles didn't make a move.

Score zero for the prospective step-mom.

I cleared my throat. "Guys, I'm sorry about the goat cheese. Didn't even occur to me that it was a weird choice. At your age I hadn't tried it either. I think my first experience with goat cheese was probably when I went to France for the first time. Funny, because it's always been around here."

Katie looked more interested when I told my story of eating goat cheese in a Paris cafe, and she spread a teensy speck onto a lavash. She sniffed it, steeled her resolve, and took a bite. She chewed and swallowed, bless her heart, and drained her water glass afterward. She managed a tiny smile.

Miles's take on the topic was different. "Goats are fun to watch. Especially the baby ones. But I'll wait until I go to France to eat goat—he paused, and swallowed with an effort—cheese." He picked up a piece of lavash and crunched into it, dry.

Both kids were being kind and making an effort. I respected them for that, and also wondered what Jared had said to them in preparation for tonight's meal. Maybe something like, "You need to at least try the food. I'm sure she won't poison us...at least, not on purpose."

I moved pans and bowls around to make space on the countertop. When I had this house built, I hadn't expected to use the kitchen for much beyond heating frozen meals and popping corn. Now suddenly I was trying to use it like a real kitchen. Kind of a stretch.

Jared pitched in to help move things around. Katie set the table, which I had intended to already have done. I showed her where the napkin rings and candlesticks were stored in an antique sideboard.

She examined the cut-glass candlesticks. "Cool. I didn't know you had stuff like this."

Jared leaned against the bar, watching Katie and then winking at me. "Carla is just full of surprises, isn't she?"

Miles's stomach growled. "Sorry."

"I apologize for the delay, Miles. Just a few minutes before we eat. Could I get you something?" I opened the fridge. "Glass of milk?"

Jared's hand was on mine, on the fridge handle. "Let me get that, okay?" He looked down into my eyes and my nervousness dissipated a smidge.

Soon we were seated at the table, passing the mixed green salad around. Miles carefully picked out a leaf of Romaine lettuce, successfully avoiding the sunflower seeds and spinach. He passed on the tahini dressing too.

"Miles, I remember once, years ago, when my brother David was about your age. Mom insisted that he try salad, and he said he would, if he could put anything he wanted on top of it. Mom agreed, and sure enough, David ate a salad that night. He never had to do it again as far as I can remember, because Mom couldn't stand to watch him pour chocolate syrup on top of a pile of greens, carrots and tomatoes."

Miles smiled widely. "That's gross." It sounded like a compliment.

I won't say the osso bucco over polenta turned out to be a hit, but at least no one spat it out. Even though all of us had taken small portions, time was required to eat the main course. For some reason it was really tough. Jared and I ate all of ours, and the kids trudged through the meat but toyed with the polenta.

"Anybody for dessert?"

Three sets of eyes met mine in a frightened question.

"Don't worry. It's just vanilla ice cream, from the store. The healthy kind, with real milk and other natural ingredients." I started to gather dishes and the rest of them jumped up to assist. "We were going to have shards of homemade peanut brittle on top of it, but...well, that didn't work out."

"Do you have chocolate syrup, Carla?" Miles asked. "Since we didn't use it on the salad."

His well-timed comment broke the stress. We all laughed together, and I pulled a jar of store-bought chocolate sauce out of the cabinet, another jar of peanuts, and one of maraschino cherries. I'm a sucker for ice cream concoctions. Good thing too, because dessert was a huge hit.

Miles pushed his dessert dish away after having thirds. "Carla, dinner was awesome. Thanks."

Katie and Jared smiled. Jared licked his spoon and leaned back in his chair, arms crossed over his stomach, looking satisfied.

Dinner had been a disaster, but still turned out okay in the end. We all worked together to clean up the kitchen, much as I protested to do it myself later. The evening ended on the patio, with Katie, Jared, and I talking about summer plans while Miles raced around with Mom's dog Daisy, who had evidently tuned into the karmic waves of having a boy within range who needed a break.

It was almost as if, just for one evening, the four of us were a family.

Chapter Seventeen

JARED CALLED ME on his way back from dropping the kids in Indianapolis for a weekend with Patty's parents.

"Hi, Jared. How are you?"

"Okay. Good. I already miss the kids." He sighed into the phone. "Weird, huh? Sometimes they wear me out, but twenty minutes into a week away from them, I feel like turning around and loading them back into the car."

"I can't exactly understand, but I know whenever Katie has been working with me for several hours and the next day she's not there, the place is painfully quiet. I realize that's not the same thing you're feeling."

"I wish you were here with me now, instead of

two hours away," he said. "I'm feeling kind of down. Maybe I shouldn't have called."

I could picture him, running a hand though his hair as he talked to me via his BMV's sound system. He'd be wearing a white shirt with a tie, probably one with a conservative diagonal stripe. The collar would be unbuttoned by now and the tie loosened. He would look tired and lonely and in need of a good wife. But was I the person to fill that role? The role of wife for him, and suitable step-mom for Katie and Miles? I loved them and didn't want to cause injury by trying to fill a void I could not.

"I'm glad you called, Jared, if talking to me makes you feel better. If I'm making you feel worse, then no, you probably shouldn't have called." I wouldn't offer unsolicited advice though. Patty's parents were insistent about their time with the kids, and Jared was the one who had to conform to what they wanted.

"I always love talking to you, Carla. You make me think about things differently, and that's a good thing. You know how it is with Patty's folks. All they have of their daughter is Katie and Miles. I get that. I really do."

"But they conveniently forget how difficult it can be for you to do things on their schedule." Jared might have taken some time off during the kids' fall break, but with them gone, there was no need.

He sighed. "Not just for me. It's not about me. The kids, you know, have friends in Serendipity now, and events they want to participate in. Oh well. I don't seem to have the guts to explain it to them. The kids are probably doing better than their grandparents about moving forward with their lives. Because of that, they don't want to complain about the visits either."

"Could you maybe invite the grandparents down here part of the time?"

"I'd be uncomfortable having them stay with us. Agatha's house can always pass a white glove test, you know. That's how Patty was too."

"Then they could get a hotel room. Or, you know what? How about suggest a weekend in one of our tiny cabins? Would they try that?"

Silence.

"Jared?"

"Sorry. I was thinking about it. First impression of the idea is they wouldn't do it. But second impression, Ted might be interested. He's into environmentalism, among other things. I'll mention it when I go up there to get the kids. Just a casual mention, to test the waters."

"Miles would encourage them, I'm sure."

"Right. He loved staying in the cabin that December before we bought our house. Katie was mortified at the lack of closet space and privacy, of course."

"Right. I remember her saying that."

"If not for you, she would have been miserable then."

"Katie was a huge help at the shop when I was making Mel's dress. She still is, when she has time and inclination."

"Carla, you've done a lot for us. I hope you realize that."

I didn't have any words. Had I helped Jared and the kids or was he just being kind?

"Thanks for answering my call. I was feeling sorry for myself, and you're the best antidote I know."

"Ah. I'm going to take that as a compliment."

"That's how it was intended." He paused, maybe deciding what he wanted to say next. "I'll be home around seven-thirty. What do you think about dinner together at the Barbeque Basement?"

"Hmm. I think it would be great food and drink, loud music, and a huge, noisy crowd. Shall I call and make a reservation for two?"

"Sounds good. I seldom go there, and never with the kids, so I'll think of it as a treat. Being there with you will make it that way for sure."

I smiled at the phone. "Now you're saying all the right things. I'll call them right away. Safe trip, Jared."

"Thanks, Carla. On second thought, would you make the reservation for eight? That will give me time for a shower before I pick you up."

"Sure. Will do."

****

When Jared arrived at my house he smelled like manly soap. I've dated guys who were really into high powered after-shave or cologne, sometimes to the point that I got a headache. But Jared just smells like Jared. Tonight he smelled like freshly washed Jared. I tried not to be obvious as I took a big inhalation when I stepped into his open arms.

He kissed me slowly and thoroughly. When we both came up for air and he loosened his hold on me, I laid my head on his shoulder. "Goodness. It's been a while since we did that."

"It sure has." He finger combed my hair, ran his hand up and down my spine. "I've missed you."

"But I've been right here. Well, I was in New York for a few days, but other than that..."

He put a finger on my lips, shaking his head. "You've seemed distant. Even that night you invited us to dinner, and worked so hard to make a meal. It was out of character for you—it was almost like spending the evening with a different woman. Except afterward when we sat out on the patio. That was the real Carla."

"Oh. The woman who doesn't cook, but can sit

on the patio like nobody's business."

"That isn't what I said, and not exactly what I meant."

"Don't you want me to cook for you?"

He shrugged. "Let's just say I'm not accustomed to it. Are you taking it up as a hobby?"

"Maybe."

He tipped his head, seeming to weigh my one-word answer. "Up to you. I've developed a workable menu schedule that involves a few easy slow cooker recipes, and a rotation of carryout food from Tony's Macaroni, Al's Place, and Chez Gwen. Katie and I take turns setting up the slow cooker. It's good experience for her. Miles takes his turn, grudgingly of course, with kitchen cleanup."

"Shouldn't be too much effort when you're getting carryout food."

"Ah, but I insist that we eat off our own plates, with actual stainless steel cutlery. Somehow it feels more civilized, and less like we're camping out."

"But I'm sure Patty always cooked a healthy dinner."

His face clouded. "Patty loved to cook. Sometimes it was healthy, sometimes not. The kids were as picky with anything new she fixed as they were with your dinner the other night. I almost told you that at the time, but didn't want to make them feel bad. It was an awkward evening for all of us, I think."

I remembered the concrete peanut brittle. "Awkward and then some."

"You didn't really answer my question. Are you taking up cooking? And if you are, is it because you want to, or because you think you should?"

"Maybe some of both. Well, actually I don't want to at all, but think I should make an effort to be more of a...um..."

"Martha Stewart?"

"Heavens no. I haven't set my sights that high."

"I think you've set them higher than that, Carla. I'm afraid you're trying to be like Patty."

"Well... I'm just trying to fit into your family. Is that wrong? Am I overstepping?" My face burned with embarrassment at the thought.

"Not overstepping. More like overthinking.

Carla, you're wonderful just the way you are. Katie and Miles and I love you. None of us expect you to replace Patty."

Did that mean I was to always be the friendly dress designer who dated the dad, provided a creative outlet and respite for Katie, and had a house near enough to a friendly dog to entertain Miles? Was that all they needed or wanted from me?

And if so, was that all I needed or wanted from them?

****

I wasn't sure how to judge the success of our evening for four at my house, except I had been exhausted by the effort of creating a meal from scratch and, even with help, the cleanup had been a major task. I'm used to sitting at a drawing table, standing cutting fabric, or sitting at a sewing machine for hours every day, and the effort made in my kitchen had been so different, it took me a couple of days to recover. Sunday is the weekly lunch at Mom's but nobody expects me to cook for that. Ever. I always take a bucket of the colonel's fried chicken, and it's usually all eaten, so why vary my routine and maybe come up with something less popular?

The fact that Jared said my cooking was basically irrelevant to him and the kids was both a relief and a disappointment. For all my talk to Mel that I wasn't sure I wanted to commit to Jared, as time went on, I found myself often imagining that it might work out. That I might be an okay step-mother. And the more I thought of the way it felt to be in Jared's arms, sharing bone-melting kisses, and even sharing ideas about how to get along with the kids' grandparents, the more I wanted that life.

Chapter Eighteen

JARED'S KID-FREE WEEK turned out to be a very big deal for the two of us. Despite the reservation I had made at the Barbeque Basement, we had opted, instead, to stay in. I called the Basement and canceled, saying I had misunderstood some plans. Besides freeing a table for other diners, I was trying to avoid busybodies creating a scenario for why we didn't show up at our appointed time. I hadn't exactly lied about having *misunderstood some plans*, because I truly believe Jared had hoped we would spend time alone instead of going out.

As usual, my freezer had a few options for dinner. Organic vegetarian enchiladas for two might not be as tasty as freshly prepared barbeque, famous Basement fries, slaw, and craft beer. But neither Jared nor I cared. We ate on the patio, with a different type of music than we would have heard at the Basement. Cicadas serenaded us, and somewhere, a hoot owl called.

Jared slid down into his chair and took a deep breath. "I could get used to this."

"Fresh country air? Dinner from the freezer?"

He reached out and took my hand. "Yes. Both of those, but more importantly, just having a quiet evening with you. We haven't had many of these."

"It always seems like a good idea to go out to eat."

"Sometimes it's a huge relief *not* to be surrounded by the people of Serendipity. The kids and I eat at home a lot. Being in our own place compared to in a restaurant dining room makes a difference in how the conversation progresses. We're much more likely to address important subjects around our kitchen table, even brought up by Katie or Miles. When we're out, Katie sure doesn't want to talk about any issue we're facing. One of the cool kids at school might overhear, I guess."

He shook his head, frowning. Jared had aged since I first met him, though it hadn't been long, time-wise. "I'm really out of my depth trying to deal with a teenage daughter. You know that. I can only hope Miles will be easier when the time comes."

"Jared, as far as I can tell, you're doing a terrific job with both the kids. For goodness sake, don't let somebody tell you that you're parenting incorrectly." I sat up, startled by the thought that occurred to me. "Are Patty's parents giving you a rough time for some reason?"

"I'll never be the person they want me to be. I never have been. Patty married me over her parents' protest, and when she was sick, even though they knew it wasn't my fault, they still blamed me. They're angry that I sold the house in Indy and moved two hours away from them. In fact, they hired a lawyer and tried to prevent me from *taking the kids away from their only support system*. Their words, obviously, not mine."

"How horrible."

"Yep. As if the kids and I needed more turmoil. We had to get out of that house, and in my opinion it was best for all of us to get out of the Indy area. Too many constant reminders of Patty. Down here, even though we're still dealing with our grief every day, it seems easier."

"Patty's parents were pretty involved with the kids when you lived up there, I guess." Maybe they had a point in trying to get Jared to find a new home nearer them.

"They're involved when it suits them. They have a very active social life. Even when Patty was sick and I could have used some predictable support from them, they couldn't be tied down. They would visit Patty and then disappear for days at a time. Katie would tell me about a Facebook post concerning a spur of the moment trip they were on."

He ran a hand through his hair. "It was a chaotic time for all of us. I think they dealt with their daughter's illness the best way they were able to. Caregiving is hard work in every possible way. They weren't up to it, not even up to sitting with Patty for a few hours. Her girlfriends did that, and I hired a home health service. Patty's friends and our neighbors were the support network the kids and I had. I think the Peabodys unrealistically expected Patty to get better. I tried to believe that as long as I could, but..." He closed his eyes, shook his head.

"Oh Jared. I'm so sorry for everything you went through. You've never talked a lot about it before."

"I didn't want to burden you. No reason to vent a bunch of negative stuff that nobody can change."

"That's not quite right. Patty's parents have the ability to change the way they relate to you. I can't imagine Katie and Miles appreciate their tactics."

"They're more positive, smiling, and encouraging when the kids are around. On the phone with me, or at times when the kids are involved in something else and the three of us are conveniently in a different part of their house, that's when they vent. The way I look at it, blaming me—punishing me—is how they're dealing with Patty's death."

"How long can they keep behaving that way?"

He shrugged, his face lined with resignation. "Forever? We're talking about two of the most stubborn people I know. Without fail, when Katie and Miles spend time with Patty's folks, some of that negativity rubs off. It can take a few days for them to get back to being themselves. I try to make it all work because they are the kids' only connection to their mom. After Patty died, her friends stopped coming around. I guess it was too painful. I've lost touch with all of them."

"Someone needs to get the grandparents to take a look at what they're doing to the kids. But you're wrong about the other thing."

"Other thing?"

"You're wrong that the grandparents are Katie and Miles's only connection to their mom. They have you, after all, and each other. Wouldn't you say the relationship the three of you have is more helpful to the kids' dealing with Patty's death and moving forward with their lives? My guess is that if the grandparents continue to be so negative, Katie and Miles won't want to go visit. So they are only hurting themselves by creating this environment in which you are painted as a villain or whatever." I touched his arm. "The kids are smart, and they know you. They were around to see who was, and who was not, helping Patty, right?"

He nodded, looking stricken at the recollection.

I slid my hand down his arm and clasped his hand with both of mine. "Jared, you're a great dad and you're raising wonderful kids. I suggest you keep on doing the right thing. Continue the visits to Indy, continue loving your children like they're the most important people in the world. And keep making a new life for the three of you. I can't imagine how hard the last few years have been. I hope it's easier now, and I hope you'll let me know how I can help, or if I stick my nose in too far, that you'll be comfortable telling me if I'm interfering."

Jared smiled, and tugged my hands, pulling me into his lap. "I can't picture you interfering. It's good to hear you say some of these things, because sometimes I wonder if you're having second thoughts about being involved with me. Since I come as part of a package deal, our relationship has surely been a massive change to your life."

I placed a soft kiss on his lips. "Dating you is certainly never dull. Who knows when we'll get a call from Katie, or need to change an evening's plan because one of Miles's rained-out soccer games is suddenly rescheduled?"

He laughed and nuzzled my neck. "I bet you wonder how you ever survived the boredom of your life before we walked into it."

I kissed him again, for a good, long time, instead of answering with words.

Chapter Nineteen

KATIE CAME INTO my shop with a face like a winter storm.

"Hi, Katie. What's wrong?"

She crossed her arms. "Nothing. I came to see if you need me to do anything."

The cute dress for her dance had turned out better that I envisioned. When it was completed, Irene showed her how to make a simple satin handbag trimmed with a cord that had previously been a belt of one of Katie's old dresses.

"Ah. Well sure, I can always use your help, honey." I smiled but it was a one-way affair. A little while later she was settled in the workroom doing some hand-beading on a turquoise, satin shawl. I took the easy chair across from her, and pulled the matching dress onto my lap. When doing hand work like this it's nice to have comfortable chairs instead of having to sit on a straight chair, as I do for the sewing machine.

We worked in silence for a while, then I had to ask some questions and see what was going on with this girl I had become so fond of. "It's been quiet here today, so I'm really glad you came in. You cheer me up."

Katie's frown didn't waver, as she focused on her work.

"Katie?"

She sighed dramatically and looked up, her quickly moving needle suddenly still. But she didn't speak.

"What's new with you, honey? I haven't had a chance to talk to you in a while."

"You had plenty of chances to talk to my dad while Miles and I were gone though, right?"

Ball in my court.

"I did see him a few times, yes. Is that a problem?"

Her slender shoulders moved in a disinterested shrug. "It's a free country, I guess."

"Last I heard, yes. But I'm wondering this: Do you want me to *not* see your dad? I hadn't gotten that feeling before."

"Are you going to marry him?"

"Well, that hasn't been decided yet. What do you think of the idea?"

She tipped her head. "Are you asking because I get to decide whether or not it happens?"

I took a breath and counted to ten. "No. Your dad and I get to decide whether it happens. But your opinion is super important. Miles's opinion too."

"He's just a baby."

"Not really. He's a smart little guy. And he misses your mom too, doesn't he?"

Her eyes misted. "I guess."

"What are your concerns, relating to your dad and me?"

She dropped the shawl into her lap and momentarily lost the needle. But she found it in the folds of the garment and held it safely. "I'm not sure.

Grandma says you're trying to push your way into our family."

"Oh."

"And she says you let me work here because it's a way to get close to Dad."

"You know that isn't true, Katie. I'm lucky to have your help whenever you have time. Does your grandmother realize what a talented seamstress you are?"

She shrugged. "I don't know. I told her I like to sew but I'm not sure she was listening. She was real angry. Her face turned red." Tears threatened, but she blinked them away. "It was Miles's fault. He told Grandma and Grandpa about the dinner you made for us. I thought it might be okay because he was giggling about the goat cheese. But Grandma didn't like it at all. It was like she suddenly felt that you were a threat. Kinda weird."

Kinda weird, but not. "Katie, I don't know how your grandma feels. I truly can't imagine what she went through when your mom was sick, and now as she's missing her only daughter." I hesitated. Katie was the closest I'd ever had to a daughter. Any time I saw her, my spirits lifted, and days without talking to her seemed cloudy. To never see her again? Unspeakable.

I cleared my throat. "Um. So, I can't see from your grandma's perspective, but I can guess since she doesn't know me, she might assume the worst. Of course she doesn't want somebody trying to take her daughter's place in the family. In your hearts." I swallowed. "Especially not somebody who would serve goat cheese to an unsuspecting little boy. That does sound pretty hard core."

Katie smiled. "Grandma has strong opinions about people. Sometimes she's not easy to like, but she does love Miles and me."

"I'm sure she does. Likely she's trying to protect you, look out for your best interest, and your dad's best interest too."

"Well, maybe. She doesn't seem to like Dad. She's always mean to him, but he is real nice back to her. And Grandpa, he just shuts it all out. He goes in another room when Grandma starts on a rant."

"Sounds like a difficult situation."

"Yeah. I wish they were nice. Our other grandparents, Dad's mom and dad, died when I was a baby."

"You're a strong girl, Katie. I'm with you, wishing things could be different with your grandparents. I was very lucky to have a grandma who lived with my family for a while when I was a little girl. Her husband had already died and she wasn't well enough to stay in her own home, so my parents moved furniture out of one of our main floor rooms and it became Grandma Standish's room. She had a little settee—like a love seat—and a pretty coffee table and lamp, her big dresser with a tall mirror, a sewing rocker, and her bed with feather mattresses on it. Oh, you've never been on anything so soft."

Katie's eyes brightened. "Your Grandma Standish was nice, wasn't she? Nice like Miss Lillian?"

I settled back, picturing my dear grandmother. "She was the sweetest lady ever. She was my dad's mother, but she was just as loving toward my mom as if she was her own daughter. And she absolutely doted on us kids."

Katie looked confused by the word.

"Doted means she paid a lot of attention to us, maybe spoiled us a bit. My sister Francie was so young when Grandma died, she doesn't remember her. Jim, David, and I took turns each day being her special helper. Like other household chores we took turns at, only different because it was a joy to do something for Grandma. She was so appreciative, but more than that, she made us feel very special because we took the time to do some small task for her." Tears burned my eyes.

"You still miss her, don't you, Carla?"

"Yes I do."

"I still miss my mom too. How long ago did your grandma die?"

"I was in kindergarten. So, a very, very long time ago. I'm sure I'll always miss her, but over time the way I miss her, and the way I think of her has changed. Funny, I can still remember she smelled like this sweet pink powder we bought from a neighbor who sold Avon. Her white hair was so soft, always pulled back in a bun at the nape of her neck. When she couldn't do her hair anymore, Mom did it for her, and sometimes she let me help. I remember wondering if a cloud could be as fluffy as Grandma's hair."

"Wow," Katie whispered. "She sounds awesome."

"She sure was."

"I have my mom's jewelry and stuff. Dad won't let me get my ears pierced until I'm sixteen." She rolled her eyes. "But once they're pierced, I get to wear Mom's earrings. Do you have anything to remember your grandma by?"

My heart hurt. "I have memories, and pictures. Sometimes that has to be enough. Grandmas are special, Katie. I sure hope your grandparents can figure out how to make their time with you worthwhile. There's time spent, and something quite different, there's time *invested*. They have an opportunity to invest time with you that you'll treasure all your life. That's what I hope will happen. Wish I could wave a wand and make it all come together the way you want it to, honey."

Her lower lip trembled and I imagine she was thinking the better use of that magic wand was a few years ago, when it could have made her mother well again. The thing was, I loved this family so much that if I could make that happen, I would, without hesitation. Even though that would mean they weren't in my life anymore.

In that moment I realized the depth of my love for Jared and his kids. If their happiness meant setting them free now, that's what I would do.

Katie and I sewed for quite some time, without interruption from any phones or customers entering the shop. It was a sweet and special time—peaceful. Evidently we had dealt with what Katie needed to address today. I felt hopeful that our friendship was reasonably solid. At last, Katie's cell rang.

"Hi, Dad. I'm at Carla's shop..." Her eyes rolled heavenward. "Okay. Yeah, I'll wait out front." She ended the call, slid the phone into her tiny handbag, and got up, carefully setting the shawl on the work table where it had been when she arrived. "Sorry I have to go. I didn't realize it's after six."

"Oh wow. Neither did I. That's the way I roll most days. Work until my stomach starts to growl." I grinned at her. "Your dad is picking you up?"

"I could walk but he worries. This time of year, it gets dark early."

"That's dads for you. If memory serves, our dad seemed old-fashioned and overprotective when I was your age. When I got older, somehow Dad got cooler."

I set the dress on the worktable too, knowing I wouldn't return to it tonight. At the front door I flipped the sign from OPEN to CLOSED. Katie stood holding the door, as a breeze played with her long blond hair.

"Thanks for talking to me, Carla."

Uncertain whether she'd be put off by my giving her a hug in the doorway where people could see, I just tucked some silky tendrils behind her shoulder. "Anytime I'm here, you're welcome, Katie. You know that, right?"

She nodded.

"You've got my cell number. Call me anytime you need to, honey. No matter what happens between your dad and me, *you*, Miss Katie Barnett, are special to me. Remember that."

Jared pulled up and waved at me. Miles waved

from the back seat. I got the idea this was a time Jared preferred to just pick up his daughter and go home. That was okay. I could afford to be patient, because I knew if Jared and I were meant to be together, that would happen somehow. If I pushed, I'd be making Mrs. Peabody's dire predictions about me seem true.

Katie's quick hug and brilliant departing smile made my day.

Chapter Twenty

JARED'S NAME AND number popped up on my cell when it rang late one afternoon.

"Hi there, handsome."

"Hey Carla. Listen, I have a problem."

"Oh. What is it?"

"There's a big wreck on I-65 and I'm halfway between exits. I have no idea when I can get home. Is there any possible way you can take care of the kids 'til I get home?"

Katie was a super responsible fourteen year old, and often had the duty of watching her brother. But I could tell Jared was in no mood to have such mundane facts pointed out to him.

I checked the wall clock. "Sure thing. It's close

to five anyway. I'll text Katie and head over to your house."

His sigh of relief was audible. "That's great. Thanks Carla. I owe you one."

I laughed. "You can be certain I'll find a way to collect. Be safe, Jared. Is there anything else?"

"Uh, not really. They'll need to eat dinner. I won't be there in time."

"Right. Got it."

When I arrived at the house, Miles was standing at the door ready to let me in.

"Hi, Miss Carla. Dad called and said you would have dinner with us, and hang out. Will you play *Donkey Kong* with me after we eat?"

Katie frowned at her brother. "Miles, give her a break. Carla doesn't know how to play video games. Not even really old ones, like *Donkey Kong*." She sent me an apologetic grin. "I don't know why Dad called you. I've got this."

I knew better than to say I had thought the same thing. Didn't want to rock the boat between father and daughter. "Oh well. I'm glad he called. Gives me a chance to, like Miles said, just hang out. First thing though is dinner. Is there anything I need to cook?"

They both look stunned and maybe a little frightened.

"No. Tonight is usually carryout from Al's Place." She opened a loose-leaf notebook and slid it toward me. The Al's Place menu was in a plastic sleeve, along with menus from other local restaurants.

"Well. That's very organized."

"Grandma says Dad is anal," Miles announced.

Nice.

"Well it's certainly handy to have everything so neat, isn't it? Let's order some food, people!"

Since it was a beautiful evening, I had the Mustang's top down. We drove through town and instead of being embarrassed about being with me, the kids were all about looking for kids they knew so they could yell and wave. At first I tried to dissuade them, but decided it wasn't hurting anything. We picked up our food and drove out to Lake Jones.

"Why not feed the ducks and geese, right? Do you come out here sometimes?"

The kids shook their heads.

"Oh. Well, I bring my lunch out here once in a while. The birds sometimes like what you bring, but sometimes are so full from other people's leftovers they don't want to eat. They'll pester you if they're hungry. Kind of need to watch the geese because they can get feisty."

Miles's brow puckered in concern. "You mean, the birds *bite*?"

"They're mostly fine. Just keep an eye on them, and absolutely don't tease them, okay?"

He nodded somberly. Katie tried to appear nonchalant but when we piled out of the car on the dock, she started breaking the bun of her sandwich into tiny bits and throwing it on the water to attract birds. I thought of mentioning the weird thing that had happened to my friend Alice at this very dock, when she was trying to get rid of that blank book that was such a problem. But I thought the tale might scare Miles, considering his immediate concern about getting bitten by geese.

We stayed at the lake longer than I had realized,

and as I waited to pull onto the highway and head back to town, my cell phone went off. So did Katie's. I didn't look at mine. I've seen too many distracted drivers, and when I'm behind the wheel I ignore whatever noise the cell might make. My phone was in my purse announcing a string of texts, and then a voice mail. There is zero cell service at Lake Jones—yet another reason to go there for a quiet respite.

"Dad sent me a bunch of texts," Katie said, scrolling through as I drove.

"Oh? What about?"

"He's home, wondering where we are. And—" her phone sang a snatch of a song by Prince. Groaning, she answered. "Hi, Dad. I—okay. Yes, right. But—. Lake Jones. Yeah. We're on our way home right now. See you in five." She jammed the phone into her handbag. "He's mad because we didn't leave a note saying where we went. He said, we could have called or sent a text. He's like, *I was worried when I came home to an empty house.* Give me a break."

Oops. I wasn't exactly scoring points with Jared tonight. Then again, it sounded to me like an overreaction. In a few minutes we were walking in through the Barnett front door. Jared was pacing the living room, running a hand through his hair which is always a sign he's upset.

Miles, bless his dear heart, ran over and gave his dad a big hug. This necessitated that Jared stop pacing. He leaned over and picked up Miles, not the easiest task these days I'd guess.

"Hey, buddy. Thanks for the hug. How was your day?"

"Good. Miss Carla got us takeout and we ate at the lake. I got to feed ducks and geese. Canada geese, Dad. You can't tease them or they might bite."

"That so? I'll keep it in mind. What else did you do today, Miles?"

The little boy shrugged. I was flattered that a simple trip to the lake was a highlight of his day. It certainly was the highlight of mine. And that included seeing the man I was in love with. Something was definitely up with Jared. He gave Miles another squeeze, blew raspberries on his cheek, and set him on the floor.

"Won't be long before you're the one picking me up, buddy." He winked at Miles.

Katie was standing with arms crossed over her chest, glaring at her dad, which couldn't be a good idea. "We were fine, Dad. Miles and I were fine before you called Carla, but once she was here and we headed out with her, we were *also* fine. Don't you trust any of us?"

Jared jammed his hands into his pants pockets. He looked more exhausted and troubled than I had ever seen him.

"It's not a matter of trust. I just worry about you guys. When I'm not here..." He shrugged and tried to smile. "I just worry. I doubt that's going to change, so you might want to get used to it."

"But we were with Carla!" Katie stamped her sneaker which was less impressive than she probably meant for it to be.

Jared glanced from Katie to me, and back again. "Yes. Something still could have happened. I texted and called both of you, with no answer."

"Jared, at Lake Jones there's no cell service. At all. Adds to the peaceful feeling of the park area." I smiled, trying to jolly him out of his mood, but his frown deepened. "Remember way back when dinosaurs roamed the earth, and we didn't even have cell phones? A person responsible for children might take them for dinner and a drive and be gone for a while. When they got back, they were back. I'm sure there's verification somewhere in the newspaper archives..."

"Carla. I'm used to knowing where my kids are. It's that simple. If you were going to take them somewhere that didn't have cell service, the least you could have done was leave a note. Remember *that* ancient technology? Piece of paper and a pointy writing instrument. Inscribe words on paper, leave it in plain sight."

"I hadn't planned ahead of time to take the lake detour. That was a spur of the moment side trip. Goodness, Jared. Please let this go."

He shook his head. "I'm glad everyone is okay. These days you just never know. It's important to me that I always know where the kids are. They're all I have."

Ah. Point taken. I didn't expect to be as

important to Jared as Katie and Miles are, but it hurt that I didn't even make the list *at all*. I swallowed my pride, or as much of it as I could manage. "I'm sorry I handled the evening badly." I picked up my handbag that I had dropped by the door when we entered. "Now that everyone is accounted for as safe and sound, I need to run. I left the shop earlier than expected when you called."

I looked apologetically at each kid in turn. "I'm glad you did call, and would be happy to come over again if you need me. But for now I'll let you get to your family evening. I'll get to work on my latest emergency ball gown." I managed to wink at Katie who smiled uncertainly.

As if in shock, she and Miles stood rooted to their spots on the living room carpet as I left, but Jared called my name as the door closed behind me. I hesitated, then hurried to my car. Jared reached it the same time I did.

"Jared, please step back. I can't open the door."

"I need to talk to you, Carla."

"Didn't seem that way a minute ago. It was

more as if you needed to talk *at* me. I'm smart enough to recognize a lack of respect when it's flung in my face. So, as I said, I'm out of here. You and your family certainly don't need me—a simpleton who can't even pull a two-hour babysitting gig without creating disaster."

"It wasn't a disaster."

"No? You sure made it sound that way. I find your reaction way, way over the top, Jared." Something in his eyes made me stop talking. Hitching my bag higher onto my shoulder, I crossed my arms. "Okay, there's more. Your diatribe wasn't just about me driving the kids to the lake, was it?"

Jared glanced toward his front door, and when he spoke his voice was low. "No, you're right. While I was sitting in that traffic jam, mentally berating myself for yet another long day away from home, I got a call." He ran his hand through his hair again. "It was an offer that would mean an end to driving hundreds of miles every week. Being home at a decent time each evening, and able to attend all the kids' events without arriving at the last minute."

"Oh. That sounds...perfect." Had the economic development committee made their decision? My understanding from this week's newspaper was that applications were still being accepted until the end of the month.

Jared nodded, still frowning. "Maybe it is perfect. A short time ago I wouldn't have considered the offer, but in the light of recent events—well, at least I didn't immediately say *no*."

"Am I allowed to know where you would be working?"

"In Indianapolis. It was my father-in-law who called. He said I would be ideal to work as his new vice president of marketing. The current guy is retiring. In their usual efficient and overbearing manner, Ted and Agatha have scoped out an appropriate house too. It's a few blocks from the elementary school, and walking distance from the soccer fields."

"Like this house, in other words."

"Yes, but no. The one he told me about is three times the size of this, in a gated community."

"Next door to the Peabody house?"

168

"Five minutes away. It would mean Katie and Miles could spend more time with family."

And zero time with the former step-mom wannabe.

"This is what you want to do?"

Jared looked deep into my eyes. "It wouldn't be my first choice, but I'm not sure what my prospects are in Serendipity."

He wasn't just talking about the economic development job either.

"I'm not sure how to fix that, Jared."

He nodded. "Right." Turning away, he walked back to the house and went in.

Chapter Twenty-One

WHEN MY BROTHER Jim walked into my shop, I knew something was up. Even though his law office is just down the block, he seldom steps foot into my *feminine lair,* as he calls it. I've always suspected he's afraid a woman will ask him if the outfit she's trying on makes her look fat.

I finished straightening the collection of fabric swatches I had pulled out for a client. "What are you doing here?"

Jim grinned. "Good to see you too, Sis." Standing near the center of the shop, he took a long visual inspection of the place. "I guess you're still keeping real busy."

I crossed my arms, waiting for him to spit out

the reason for his visit. "Yes, the place is successful, and I'm swamped as usual. Anything I can do for you, Jim? Or are you going around to store owners on the square doing a survey on the state of our business?" A thought occurred to me. "That's right, you're on the economic development committee, aren't you?"

His face colored. "Unfortunately, I couldn't get off the committee when recent events made my seat there more than a little uncomfortable."

"Oh? How's that?" I decided he might talk more if encouraged. "And—would you like something to drink? I have a pitcher of sweet tea in the fridge, and some bottled water."

He followed me past the drapes. "Glass of tea sounds great." Looking relieved to be out of the showroom area, he leaned against a wall in the workroom while I put ice cubes into a glass and poured tea. He took a long drink, then swirled the glass, letting the cubes make a melodic sound bouncing off the sides. Trying to get up his nerve to say something, I assumed.

Finally, he cleared his throat. "Thing is, Carla, I'm in the middle of something I didn't want to be part of. I'm talking Jared's application to be director of economic development for the county, in case you hadn't guessed."

"The possibility occurred to me that you might be talking about that. Heaven forbid you come right out and tell me. That would be just boring."

He smiled crookedly. "Yeah. Well, like I said, I'm in the middle and don't want to be. When Jared applied, I told the committee I felt like I ought to resign because I didn't think it would look good for me to vote."

"Because you're likely to vote for him, or against him?"

He shrugged. "I didn't state that to the committee, and I won't state it to you either. Ethics, Carla. My concern was simply how it would look to citizens for me to vote at all. It was suggested that I abstain instead of resigning from the committee."

"That's stupid. Either they want your input, or they don't."

"That's kind of what I thought. That committee, and the director position, are so important to our community, if we're ever to grow in a sustainable way." He gulped some tea. "So I'm staying on, to try to help make a positive difference."

I sat down, bracing myself for whatever he was here to tell me that I was probably not going to like. "I agree with you. Serendipity has a lot of untapped potential. So far the series of directors hasn't seemed as interested in tapping the local potential as they have in building up their own resumes by courting whatever shiny opportunity comes along. Jim, are you here to tell me something about Jared's chances of getting the job?"

"No. I just want you to know I'm going to do the right thing, as I see it. We have some resumes, and we'll carefully go over and discuss those and whatever else might arrive by the deadline. Do interviews."

I nodded. "Good. Do it the right way, hire the best person. I won't try to sway you. As if I could."

He smiled, then drained his tea and set the glass on the counter by the sink, with a clink of ice cubes. "I'm glad we understand each other, Carla. You know I always want what's best for you, right?"

I tried to read a meaning behind those words. "You're my big brother and take that job very seriously. Jim, I trust you. Jared and I will be fine, no matter what happens with the directorship." Smiling as sincerely as possible since I wasn't sure what I had just said was the truth, I reached out and took Jim's hand.

Jim squeezed my hand back. "Thanks for the tea, and the talk. See you at lunch on Sunday."

After he left I sank onto a couch in the showroom. Jim is one of the most ethical people I know. As an attorney, he's used to keeping his mouth shut about matters that aren't public information. I knew he would do what he thought was right, once all the resumes had been reviewed and the best candidates interviewed. But Jim has a long memory when it comes to wrongs done, particularly relating to family. Jared's introductory visits to Serendipity a few years ago had resulted in distress and bad feelings, and Jim held onto that grudge longer than the rest of the Standish family. I wasn't sure if he had completely let go of it.

Did I really want Jared to be the economic development director for my county? He was such a recent transplant; could he be as effective as someone who was either originally from Serendipity, or had been economic development director in another community? I understood that Jared wanted to work closer to home, for the sake of his time with the kids. And high paying jobs in Serendipity aren't plentiful. From what I had read, the position offered a good salary and benefits package, though probably much less than he was used to earning.

My concerns were two-fold. If Jared were selected, would he like the job and be happy in his new status as cheerleader of our small town? The other side of it was, if he got the job, would the locals support him or pick at every move he made? The only good person we'd had as economic development director had been gossiped about, bad-mouthed, and generally pecked to death until he resigned. He moved out of town and, I suppose, shook the dust off his feet at the city limits.

I didn't blame the guy either. Serendipity is my home and I love it, but the small-mindedness can be maddening. I'm fortunate to live and work here, yet travel quite a bit, and interact with all kinds of people.

If I only had the local shop with local patrons, I'm not sure I could stand the limitations.

In Jared's current work, he interacted with people all over the state. I understood the driving could be wearing, especially in bad weather. And I got that he wanted to be available when the kids needed him. But would he like having Serendipity not only as his residence, but also as his employer? Would it be terribly limiting to think about our little corner of the universe all the time?

Maybe that was really my biggest concern about the E.D. job. Maybe I was afraid if Jared were hired, his world would shrink, and mine might be expected to shrink right along with it.

Chapter Twenty-Two

ONE SATURDAY AFTERNOON I heard a soft knock on my front door. I looked out the top half glass and almost missed seeing the person who had knocked—my nephew Matthew. I threw the door open, delighted to see the little guy, who at eight years of age has better things to do than spend time with a boring aunt who doesn't bake cookies or drive a truck. (Although driving a truck, even one with a manual transmission, wasn't difficult, it wasn't my choice of ride. Same with the tractor that's been on the farm all my life. But I'll leave the cookie baking to Mom, or Emily, or anybody.)

"Hey, Matthew!" I saw his best buddy standing to the side, where I hadn't noticed him earlier. "And hey there, Miles! What brings you boys to my door today? Selling something for school?"

They both shook their heads no, their faces stone serious.

"Aunt Carla, Miles is spending the day with me. I told him it was okay if we come down and talk to you about something. It's important."

Miles's expression didn't change. I hadn't seen him this tightly wound since they first moved to town.

I stepped further back into my living room. "Sure thing, guys. Come on in and we'll talk. Could I get you something? Chocolate milk?" Fortunately milk and chocolate syrup are always on hand.

The two exchanged looks. "Yes ma'am," Miles said.

I motioned for them to follow me to the kitchen. "Oh my. That's awfully formal, isn't it, Miles?"

"I'm not sure what to call you, Miss Carla."

"Well, that'll do. It's worked for us up until now, right?" I winked at him, then took down glasses, filled them with milk, and stirred in chocolate. When I looked up, the boys stood watching me. It was eerie to see zero animation on those two young faces.

"So. Sit in here, or out on the patio?"

"Patio's good," Matthew said. That was no surprise, as he loved being out on the farm as much as his father had at that age.

I handed a glass to each of them and opened the door. "Patio it is." They went outside and I quickly stirred up the same concoction for myself, and joined them. A moment later we were seated around the wrought iron table, sipping.

Although their behavior had me worried about the visit, I leaned back and tried to get comfortable. A light breeze brought a whiff of pine to my nostrils, always a relaxing sensation. "What is the important thing you need to discuss with me?"

"Miles and me thought you were going to be his step-mom, Aunt Carla. We were counting on it. Now his dad says they might move to Indianapolis, and live by Miles's Grandma and Grandpa Peabody. Miles says if they move there, you won't go with them, because his grandma and grandpa won't let you. I told him you can move there if you want to, because nobody's going to tell you what to do."

Matthew shot a look to Miles, who nodded. Then Matthew continued, "But I thought you were always going to live here on the tree farm with our family. Even though you travel sometimes, I thought you always like to come home." His voice started to waver and he halted, looking out briefly toward the forest of evergreens. "I wouldn't ever want to live someplace else. This is the most awesome place in the world."

Matthew had lived in an apartment in Fort Wayne, until Melissa bought the big house on Serendipity's Main Street when he was four years old. When he was six, and Melissa and Jim got married, they moved into Jim's cabin on the farm. Not exactly a lot of experience behind his statement of the tree farm being the most awesome place in the world. But as it happened, he was right.

I managed some kind of a smile. "I must agree with you about living here on the farm, Matthew." I reached over and took his hand, and with my other hand got Miles's. "As to Jared's decision about moving, that's for him to make, isn't it? He has to do what he thinks is best for you and Katie."

My eyes held Miles's as tightly as my hand was holding his. "Miles, if your dad decides to move your family up to Indianapolis, that's—you know—not something I can interfere with." I squeezed both hands and gently let go, tried to assume a relaxed posture even though the conversation had me on edge. I didn't need to upset the boys even more by letting them see how emotionally wrought up I was.

"Sorry, guys, but I'm limited here. I know you're best friends, and I would hate to see you separated by a two-hour drive. I can sort of relate, because one of my best friends moved away, and it took her years to come back."

Matthew nodded. "My mom."

"Yes. So even though I can kind of understand what you might be feeling, I can't really help with your problem."

"Miss Carla, you could marry my dad. Then he would have to keep living here. Matthew and me could still be best friends."

Here we go. How to explain the vagaries of adult relationships?

"Miles, honey, getting married is a very big decision. Your dad and I are more like really good friends."

"I don't think so," Miles said. "He doesn't seem to like you very much right now."

I croaked out a laugh. "Well, there you go. I guess we just *used* to be good friends, then." I hoped I wouldn't start to cry because I had an idea it wouldn't take a lot to get the two of them shedding tears too.

"I think you should marry him, Miss Carla. Since you guys had that fight about us going to the lake, he's been really sad. He doesn't smile very much, and when he does, it's not a real smile. Katie showed him that dress the lady helped her make at your shop. At first he was really mad, mostly at you, but then Katie said she couldn't wear the dress from Grandma Peabody because it was just like our mom's dress."

"It—what?"

"There's a picture in our living room of our mom wearing a dress that same color. Katie feels like crying whenever she sees the dress from Grandma Peabody. She said it's like they don't even like her for being Katie. But I think they just really like that picture of our mom, and didn't do it on purpose."

No wonder Katie had been so adamant about needing something different. I could picture her opening the package from her grandmother and seeing that physical reminder of her mother's death. Thank goodness that, with Mom's idea, and Irene's willingness to help, we had done something positive—a creative project that Katie had learned from, while also getting some mentoring. Irene was just as great a teacher and seamstress now as when I'd had her in school.

"Katie and me are doing stuff to make him happier about living here in Serendipity instead of moving, but I don't think it's working. He wants that new job of development director or something. He says if he gets that, we will probably stay. But if he doesn't, we probably have to move. Katie says Dad is pulled in too many directions. But I'm not sure what she means. I just know he's not happy."

He wiped chocolate milk off his upper lip. "We're all sad sometimes because my mom died. We can't help that, Miss Carla. I was too little, and now I have a hard time remembering her. I have to watch a video or look at pictures. But I know Mom can't come back and be with us like a person, even though a little bit of her is still here with us. So I think you should marry my dad and make us a family again. That's what we all need. You used to be happy when you were with us, didn't you?"

I nodded, unable to deny it. "But it's not really that simple, Miles."

"Yes it is, Aunt Carla," Matthew said. "Grandma Lillian always says love is the most important thing in the world. So if you love Miles and Katie's dad, and if he loves you, then you should get married and be a family. You're always grumpy since you had that fight with Miles's dad, and he's grumpy too." Matthew sighed hugely and rolled his eyes. "I don't know why you grownups are making it so hard. Us kids are about worn out with the drama."

I managed not to laugh out loud at Matthew's

declaration. The situation between Jared and me, and the question of whether or not he got the E.D. job, wasn't that simple. If only it were.

Chapter Twenty-Three

ALTHOUGH I DIDN'T expect it to make much difference, I thought I owed it to Matthew and Miles to at least speak to Jared about their concerns. I texted him when I knew the kids would be at school. I asked if he was home, and whether I could come over and talk, and he agreed.

Jared met me at his front door. "Let's walk," he said, pointing at the community trail just across the street.

"Oka-aay." I swiveled around and followed him. Thank goodness I'd been planning a stop at the recycling trailer next, and was wearing sneakers. We crossed the street and turned toward the elementary school. "So. This is nice." I cleared my throat. "You're probably wondering why I called you here," I joked.

Jared shot me a look. "I wonder why you do a lot of things, Carla."

"Really? I didn't know I was such a hardship on you."

He held up both hands and faced me, causing me to stop too. "I hope you're not here to start another fight, or build on past ones. I was hoping for a truce."

"I guess we've been having a truce, considering that we haven't talked *at all* in a few days."

"Thought you were done with me," he muttered, turning left off the street, and taking the trail that leads along the north line of the elementary school grounds.

"Yes. Well, that goes both ways. You obviously don't need or want me to be part of your family." A memory of Miles's distraught face flashed into my mind. Poor little guy was wishing for something that wasn't going to happen. Or if he was going to have a step-mom, it wouldn't be me. That much was clear.

"Whatever it is that you have to say, please get to the point. I have to meet some people."

"Oh, you're so busy, aren't you? As it happens,

I have a business to run, and I need to be there to open in a little while. Yet I've taken time out of *my* schedule to talk to you about your son."

Jared stopped dead and faced me. "What about Miles?"

"He's upset. He doesn't want to move away from Serendipity and his friends. It's not about me, Jared. I understand that whatever was between you and me is over." Had my voice wavered when I said that? Probably just because I was out of breath from the pace. "But are you carefully considering all the possibilities of the job opportunity and move? I understand your concerns about being on the road—"

"No you don't. You can't possibly empathize with me."

I decided not to touch his statement which was a slam against me as a woman with no kids. "I understand you want to spend all the time you can with Katie and Miles. I *do* understand that. They're awesome kids. Lord, how I miss having Katie around like she was for a while. Miles and I don't have that much in common, but he's such a sweetheart. I look at his face, hear his concerns about moving away from his best friend, and I can relate, because I lost Mel for several years. Even though we were done with high school when she decided to leave Serendipity forever, it broke my heart. We kept in touch, but when she wasn't here in town it simply was not the same. Having her back was like having myself all in one piece again." Of course now that Alice had married Robert and moved to the west coast, I was back to feeling ripped apart.

"Thinking of you moving your family reminds me of my own loss." *Because if you leave, you'll take my heart.* I couldn't say that to him and make the situation be about me. Maybe I tend to be wrapped up in myself, but right now my concern was for the kids.

Jared started walking again, turning off the paved path onto the grassy one cut through a large field, used for cross country team practice. "The only way I can see staying here is if that economic development job comes through."

"Are you sure? Maybe something else will come along."

"I can't imagine a position in Serendipity that

would be as good a fit for me."

I sighed. "You really have your heart set on this."

He nodded. "I've been through years of back issues of the local paper to get an idea of where Serendipity has been. On first sight it looks like this little paradise, but the deeper you dig, the more problems become apparent. Complicated problems at that."

I was impressed. "Years of back issues? That sounds deadly dull."

"Some of it, but a careful reading can be very informative. Patterns are apparent. Patterns including some local leaders making what I would call poor decisions." He shook his head. "Not all the messes can be reversed, but some of them can."

"And you would want to beat your head against that wall? Because you know, if you're trying to change patterns, we're not really into that."

"Believe me, I realize. You're an example of the hard-nosed attitude around here. I still can't get the picture out of my mind, of when I told you someone had suggested I apply for the E.D. job. You were horrified."

"I certainly was *not*. I was just surprised."

"After reading about financial mismanagement at the hospital, and what it took to save the facility, I understand a little bit of why some people would hesitate to trust an outsider in another position of leadership. *Some* people, Carla. But not you. The fact that you don't support me is another situation entirely. If a relationship isn't built on trust, there's no chance for it to thrive. I suppose we're better off to realize now."

"I do trust you, Jared. And anyway, I'm not on the committee. I don't have a vote about you getting the job or not."

"I'm not so dense as to believe that, Carla. In this community, most decisions are made outside of any meeting room. Your lack of support is apparent, and that's going to communicate itself to the people who do the actual voting." He shook his head. "The fact that Jim's on the committee bothered me at first, but he's fair."

"And I'm *not*?" I looked around, since I had spoken louder than I'd intended. But we were in the middle of the field.

Jared shook his head. "I don't know why you distrust me, Carla. I guess I was an idiot to ever believe the two of us could have a future together. We're just too different." We had arrived at Shelby Street again, a few yards from his driveway. A sleek silver Cadillac was sitting in it, next to my Mustang. As we approached, an impeccably dressed and coiffed man and woman emerged. They looked like an advert for retiring with wealth.

Jared's voice was low. "Patty's parents. They're here to talk about the move to Indianapolis."

Chapter Twenty-Four

THE NEWSPAPER SAID that, due to the importance of the E.D. job to our community, the public was invited to the five interviews that would be conducted. It wasn't clear how many applications had been received, but Jared's name was among the five. Each person under consideration had a small bio in the paper.

One candidate was a former E.D. in a county about 100 miles north of us, which admittedly is much more prosperous than our county. It also has a different demographic, containing three of the most populous and affluent cities in the state. I wondered how anything that worked there would translate here.

The second candidate had credentials that looked as if they belonged on a Fortune 500 profile. My mind immediately grabbed the saying, "If it sounds too good to be true, it probably is."

The third person was Tony, the owner of Tony's Macaroni, local pizzeria extraordinaire. What I knew about him was that he could make an awesome pizza, and he and his wife drove their big RV to southern Texas each fall, where they lived for six months. That schedule didn't seem conducive to being a hands-on development director.

Darlene Kincaid, local businessperson who also has a successful interior design shop in neighboring Mendacious, had thrown her tasteful hat into the ring and was the fourth candidate. Darlene is an aunt to my sister-in-law Emily. So if anyone had worried about Jim being swayed by family ties, they should worry instead about which way he could sway. Darlene, for all her talents, isn't known for her ability to play well with others.

Jared rounded out the list of five, with his background of working within many Indiana communities in all facets of real estate and land development.

Just from reading the article and looking at the photos, it was obvious to me that Jared should be chosen for the job. The first guy looked shifty-eyed, and the second one reminded me of a boy in high school who has spent most of his years since in a variety of penal institutions, for theft. But a person shouldn't judge a book by its cover, so I decided to attend the committee's interviews. I knew Jared might not consider it a vote of support, but it was.

On the day of the interviews, I put up a sign on my front door that I use when I'm out of town. *Sorry Creations is closed today. Please stop back and see us on____.* I filled in *Tuesday* written on a sticky note. Let no one say I put on airs.

I drove to the county office building, and went in the downstairs door to the meeting room. The committee members were seated at a table in the front of the room. Jim nodded at me, and I took a seat toward the back. A few others straggled in. Someone put a gentle hand on my shoulder, and I turned around. It was Mom.

"Hi, honey. I'm going to sit nearer the front.

Join me?"

I didn't want to, but picked up my handbag and followed her. She sat, and I dropped into the chair next to her. "Mom, front row? Yikes."

She shrugged. "I want to be able to see and hear, don't you?"

I leaned over to whisper into her ear. "I don't want to make Jared nervous. I'm afraid when he sees me..." *Maybe he'll take it as a sign of support, or perhaps quite the opposite.*

Mom patted my arm. "Carla, you worry too much. Jared will be pleased to see you here. It will give him just the nudge he needs."

"Nudge?"

"You know, *nudge.* The two of you have been doing this dance of off-and-on courtship. Your being here for him today makes it obvious exactly where your heart lies."

It does? I didn't say it out loud, but Mom still nodded. Someone closed the back doors, and the E.D. committee chair called the meeting to order. In a dispassionate voice she stated our reason for being here, and that each candidate would be brought in separately. They were waiting in a room down the hall. She asked one of the other committee members to bring the first candidate in. Just as the candidate from the big county up north entered through the side door, the back door opened and closed too. I turned around, interested. My blood froze when I recognized the couple who slipped into the back row. It was Patty's parents. They surely weren't here in a show of support for Jared, were they? How had they learned about the meeting in the first place?

****

I was surprised that the audience was allowed to ask questions of each candidate, after the committee had exhausted their own. But I wasn't surprised that the only question from the audience was, "How would you bring more jobs to Serendipity?"

Each candidate had his or her own unique way of side-stepping the issue. By the time Candidate Number Five, Jared, entered the room, the audience was shifting around, seeming bored with the proceedings. If I had to choose from among the first four, I would have chosen Darlene Kincaid, yet I knew she didn't have the interpersonal skills to work well with current or potential business owners, or other community leaders.

Jared came in looking tired. Had he been awake all night worrying about this? He saw Mom first and returned her smile. I smiled too, and he seemed to perk up a bit. Once he was seated and looked out at the small assemblage, I knew the moment he spied Mr. and Mrs. Peabody. He stiffened and looked down at the table. Shame on them for putting him in such a situation. They weren't here to support him, but to hope he failed and would have to move his family to Indy.

The committee members asked Jared the same questions they had asked everyone else, and his answers were on point and showed a level of knowledge—a clear understanding of both the responsibilities of the job and needs of our community—that no one else had come close to. When they finished the set of questions everyone else had answered, and Jared had knocked each one out of the park, one of the members cleared his throat and did what I had been afraid of.

He painted a picture from Serendipity's first experience with Jared Barnett. Then he asked why the committee should trust Jared with the job of representing and leading our community into the future.

Jared's face turned redder as the damning information was shared. By the time the question was asked, I didn't know if Jared would storm out of the room (I wouldn't have blamed him) or blow up (also not an unreasonable response).

Jim spoke up. "Hal, I'd say that incident is best left in the past. My family and I have moved on."

Hal wasn't having it. He tapped his pen on the plastic table, staring at Jared and waiting for what he would say. It was one of those moments in which the stress hanging in the air was a palpable thing. I wanted to say something in Jared's defense, but didn't know if speaking up would help or hurt him.

Mom stood up. "Hal, I can speak to your—I'm not sure if we should call it a question to Jared, or an accusation. But I can certainly state without reservation, as the owner of one of the oldest businesses in our community, that the Standish family Christmas tree farm was not only unharmed by anything Jared ever did or said, but we have flourished as an indirect result. Jared's original concept of developing the land was a good one. I wasn't ready to let go of the tree farm, and still am not, so the timing wasn't right for us.

"I'm afraid our community tends to immediately shut down anyone with a new way of looking at situations, which is part of why we've seen a big net loss in local employment in the last twenty years. But because Jared believed so strongly in the potential for people coming to the Serendipity area for relaxation, as you know we now have a thriving bed and breakfast business on the farm.

"I have no hard feelings toward Jared—quite the contrary. I'm thrilled to have him and his little family here in our community. We need new blood, not a constant recycling of the same negative attitudes. I don't have a vote, of course, and didn't come here intending to make a speech. But when someone is being treated wrongly, I can't just stand by and let it happen. I won't be a party to that type of treatment, and neither should any of you." She pointed at each committee member as she said her last sentence.

Hal had the grace to look sheepish, and he withdrew his question.

Mom sat down. "Did I come on too strong?" she whispered.

I reached over and squeezed her hand. "You're fantastic."

The single audience question was asked again, but instead of trying to avoid giving a direct answer, Jared talked with confidence about the strengths of our citizenry, but also the difficulties we're up against in trying to bring new employers to the town.

"We won't see a return to the days of having several manufacturing plants here. There are some options though. None of them is easy, but with additional training and if possible some grants..."

I accidentally tuned out of what he was saying. I was just in awe of the man, his honesty, and willingness to bravely meet a challenge. I thought I heard the back doors open and close.

Jared was excused, and the meeting ended shortly after that, with the chair announcing a decision would be made by Friday. I couldn't imagine that, once they had met in private, it would take more than a minute to take a vote and choose Jared. He was by far the best candidate. Mom and I left together, and it was without surprise that I noted the Peabodys were nowhere to be seen.

Chapter Twenty-Five

I WASN'T SURE if I was a masochist for doing it, but I sat in my car in the parking lot after the meeting, waiting for Jared to emerge. When he walked out with his briefcase, he didn't notice me, so I got out and met him at his car. He seemed startled at my presence, but thank goodness he smiled.

"Jared, I just have to tell you how terrific you were in there. Your answers were so much better than anyone else's. Obviously all your hours of homework paid off."

He ran a hand through his hair. "Paid off in knowledge, at least. We'll see what the committee decides about the job. They got all five of us candidates together after the audience left, and said we would be hearing the decision in the next few days."

"I hope you get the position. I know I stuck my foot in my mouth about it before, but... Okay, I already told you how great you were in the interview. I also need to tell you how great you are as a person. And how very much I miss you."

His eyes bore into mine. "Is that right?"

"Yes," I whispered.

"Then I guess it's okay to admit that being without you has been driving me mad, Carla. I haven't slept a full night since the last time we argued. The kids kept trying to get me to apologize to you, beg you to take me back. They seem to think I'll never be happy unless you and I get married."

"Oh. Well, that's kind of a big deal isn't it?"

"To have both of them agree is a big deal. To have them insisting I re-marry seems almost a miracle. You know we all still have times that we grieve for Patty."

"Yes. I expect you always will, though they'll likely change over time."

He kissed both of my palms. "You understand

about loss. The fact that you haven't pushed me to *grieve faster* has been a gift, you know. Everything about you is perfect for me, Carla. For Miles and Katie, too."

"Because I'm not trying to be Patty? Except for that singular kitchen fiasco, I mean."

He nodded. "Because you don't try to be her, because you don't attempt to push our memories of her away, and because you, Carla Standish, are an amazing woman. I fell in love with you the first time we met, you know."

"Is that right? I guess I kind of fell in love with you then, Jared, but I was scared. I have a horrible track record with men, and none at all with step-kids."

"I'm hoping we can put all talk of track records behind us." He pulled me into his arms and kissed me, then, sighing, slid his hands down my arms. "Guess this isn't the ideal place—" His cell phone vibrated and he huffed out a breath. "Doesn't seem to be the time either. The Peabodys are calling. I suppose I should answer." He mostly listened for several minutes.

"They're at my house. I should go and try to

calm them down a little. If I heard right, they stopped in for a coffee after leaving the meeting, and your mom dropped by when she left here. From what I understand, she very sweetly explained to them that they need to let me raise my own children in the way I see fit. And she expounded a bit on the joys of grandparenting, and how wonderful it would be for both Miles and Katie to have a second grandmother—her. She said she would keep in touch with them and make sure they know about the kids' special programs because Serendipity's schools are so great... Did your mom ever work in P.R.?"

"Every day of her life. Public relations for Dad, for the farm, for us kids, for school when we didn't want to go. For a little lady she has loads of spunk."

"I'll say. The Peabodys have never listened to me, or respected me. But your mom, as a grandparent and maybe more importantly as a successful businesswoman, seems to have gotten through to them." He shook his head, astounded.

"How could you work for him, Jared, if he doesn't listen to you?"

Jared nodded. "You're right. I already told Ted

that I couldn't take his very generous offer, and we wouldn't be moving to Indianapolis. Serendipity is our home. The three of us love it here. Somehow I'll find a job that will allow us to stay. I can't imagine wanting to raise my kids anywhere else." He kissed the tip of my nose. "Sorry I have to go. May I call you later?"

"I'll count on it."

Chapter Twenty-Six

THAT SUNDAY, THE Barnett family joined us for lunch. We all wanted to be together, to celebrate Jared's selection as the new county Economic Development director. After the meal, Mom brought a triple-layer Swedish nut cake into the dining room.

"No candles for a new job cake, Jared," she explained. "You'll be dealing with plenty of hot air once you start work."

Emily stood by Mom, passing each dessert plate as Mom cut the cake. "I'm so glad they chose you, Jared. Now I have some hope that Serendipity will be flourishing by the time the next generation is ready to take over."

"That's a big compliment, Emily. I've got a

couple of decades before you take me too much to task on behalf of your baby, right?"

"Maybe less, if he or she is a prodigy who wants to start a business as a teenager."

David put his arm around his wife's still-tiny waist. "That would be cool. Or maybe our little genius will come up with better ways to run the Christmas tree farm. I'd be good with that."

The conversation headed into a few other directions, and in a lull after eating the cake, Jared asked me to go outside with him.

Knowing the air was cool and crisp, I grabbed my wool sweater and Jared pulled on his jacket before leaving the house. So much had happened this autumn, which had made the time pass more swiftly. Christmas tree season would be here in just a few weeks.

Jared took my hand and led me off the front porch, around to the back of the house.

"It's probably impossible, but I thought we might have a moment of privacy back here. Carla, I need to ask you a couple of questions. First, are you afraid of being a stepmother?"

I took a deep breath. "Yes, because it's a huge step for all of us. But...I hope we could all learn to adjust."

"You're right there. We will adjust. The kids love you. You know that, right?"

Yes, I did. Miles, Katie, and I had been through some adventures lately, and had bonded in a way I never expected. I nodded. "I love them too, in case that was going to be your next question."

Jared winked. "I would never have expected to date a woman who jets to Cannes to adjust a hemline for a glamorous star's evening gown. Nor would I have expected to date a woman who is as glamorous as the stars whose hems she adjusts." He kissed my palm. "I'm almost afraid to ask the second question, but I'll go crazy if I don't. Plus my kids will disown me." Jared cleared his throat, and positioned himself on one knee. Looking up into my eyes, he asked, "Carla, would you do me the immense honor of being my wife?"

At first I couldn't speak, I was so overcome by emotion. "Jared, I do love you. And I love Katie and Miles. I'm thrilled for you to propose. I just—" I hesitated.

"What? What is it? Something I've done?"

"No! Not at all. Something *I* have done." I sank down next to him on the grass. "Years ago my Grandma Standish gave me her engagement ring. I foolishly lost it. You'll think I'm silly, because I was very young. Yet all my life I had the idea that I could never find my own happily-ever-after because of that mistake."

His reaction was slight; just a raised eyebrow.

I continued. "All these years I knew there was no way I could find a forever love like Grandma and Grandpa had, because I had ruined it by playing with that ring, and losing it."

He kissed my forehead as we knelt there in the grass. I wondered if anyone in the house was looking out Mom's kitchen window. If they were, we would be in for a good old-fashioned teasing in a few minutes. I could only hope no photos showed up on Facebook.

"You lost your grandmother's ring and have been upset about it for...how long?"

"Let's just say decades."

He shook his head, grinning. "Cutting edge fashion designer balanced with old-fashioned sentimentality. Quite a combination."

"Well. You never know about people, I guess."

He nodded. "Evidently. So the only thing that would make this moment perfect is..."

His attention swung away from me for a moment. He blinked, reached out and picked up something that was embedded in the grass.

"Carla?" Jared held it out to me. Grandma Standish's ring.

I jumped up, shocked. "Jared! Where did that come from?"

"I just saw the sun reflecting on it." Jared's face was calm but surprised. "Is this the ring you were talking about? How could it have been here all these years?"

I sank back down onto the grass next to him. "I'm not sure why anything would surprise me these days. After what happened with Matthew, and Emily's miracle that brought her and David together. And then Alice and Robert..."

My voice trailed off as it started to tremble. This was my sign. This was what I had hoped for, the answer to so many years of prayers. The man I loved, and the ring that was promised to me, ensuring happiness.

I took his free hand in both of mine. My tears flowed, transforming the scene into a romantic watercolor. "I can't tell you how many times I've looked for it. I guess it was here for you to find. This is just the most recent way you have changed my life for the better. I'm so grateful."

He pulled me into his embrace, and we sat together on the grass. After he pushed a strand of hair away from my ear, he whispered, "I'm honored to be the man who found the ring for you. I'll get used to coincidences like this after a while, I suppose." He kissed my cheek and I snuggled further into the circle of his arms.

He turned the ring in his fingers; its sparkle seemed brighter than last time I'd seen it.

Jared said, "The first time I drove into Serendipity, I knew there was something special about this town. Back then I didn't expect to make a new life here with the kids. And in my wildest dreams I wouldn't have imagined holding you in my arms, Carla." He paused, and sat up straighter. "Now, back to what I brought you out here for: Will you marry me?"

"Yes," I breathed. Jared slid Grandma's ring onto my finger.

Chapter Twenty-Seven

JARED DROVE TO The Jewelry Box when his work day was done. I walked down from my shop, and was pleased to see Katie and Miles when I entered the lovely little jewelry store.

"Hey, guys! This is a fun surprise. Thanks for coming along today."

Miles huffed out a big breath. "Dad made us."

Jared chuckled and he and I shared a brief kiss. I leaned over so I could look directly into Miles's eyes. "You know, I thought that might be the case. But I'm still super glad you're here. If we're all lucky, your dad and I will find the rings we want right away. Then we can celebrate at the soda fountain down the block, right?"

Jared's eyebrows shot up. "Carla, that sounds like bribery."

"Okay, it is, a little bit. Whatever helps us shop efficiently."

Katie's face was bright with enthusiasm. "I can't wait to see what you pick out to go with your grandma's ring, Carla." She took my left hand in both of hers to look again at Grandma Standish's ring. "It's so cool. The whole story is awesome."

I nodded, steering her toward the closest case so I could start shopping. "You'd think, with all the surprising things my family has had happen to them, having this ring back wouldn't be a big deal. But honestly, I still get shivers when I think how your dad just leaned over and plucked it out of the grass."

Chip, the owner and jeweler, finished a phone call telling a customer what time the store closed today. Then he met us at the jewel case. "Afternoon, Carla. I hear you've got an engagement ring."

"Hey, Chip. Right, word travels fast and all that." I pulled off the ring and set it on the plate glass.

"It belonged to Grandma Standish."

Chip swiveled the loupe down and examined it. "Nice little diamond. Good fire." He handed it back.

"I'm looking for a very simple wedding band. Honestly, just a thin gold band like Grandma wore would be ideal." I looked up at Jared who was now standing beside me. "And Jared is going to choose something too."

Chip slid a panel sideways and reached into the case. He set a small powder blue velvet box on the surface in front of me. "Is this what you're looking for?"

"Yes, exactly." I picked up the band and slid it onto my ring finger. "It's big though."

Chip stepped away and returned with a sizing tool—a stainless steel ring with a couple dozen other rings hanging from it. "Let's get your size." He held out one of the rings and I slid my finger into it. The stainless steel fit—not too tight or too loose.

"That's perfect. You're kinda good at this." I chuckled as Chip pulled a pad of paper over and wrote my name and ring size on it.

He chuckled. "After forty years, I should be decent at judging sizes. You want to look at some others?"

I shook my head. "Nope. This is just what I wanted. Everything else looks fancier."

He shrugged. "It's cyclical. Right now most women want lots of diamonds on the wedding band." He shifted his gaze to Jared, smiling. "Okay, pressure's on you. Are you going to be as decisive as your fiancée?"

Jared was leaning over looking into the case. "We can only hope. Um, could I see those two?" He pointed at some rings in boxes near him. Miles was plastered up against Jared, suddenly interested in the proceedings. His eyes followed Chip's every movement as he retrieved the boxes, slid both of them across the counter to Jared.

About twenty minutes and a dozen rings later, Chip had put both of our selections into a little envelope marked with our names, phone numbers, and ring sizes. "Should have these by the end of this month. Unless you're on a tight schedule like Jim and Melissa were."

I held up both hands in self-defense. "Heavens, no. We're not sure of a wedding date yet, but no way am I putting myself and everyone else through that. Besides, it has to be a day that works for the whole family." Katie smiled and kissed my cheek, before moving out of the circle to look at something else.

Jared laughed and put his arm around my shoulders. "Yep. Basically there's no telling, Chip. If we need a rush put on those, we'll let you know, okay? I guess in a pinch we could use the Claddagh." Jared indicated it and Chip's eyes followed the movement.

"That's interesting," he said. "Another old family piece?"

I shook my head. "No. It was recently given to me by a friend." I slid the ring off and handed it to the jeweler. "I brought it in to ask your opinion."

Chip swiveled the loupe down again, and looked. "Hmm." He glanced up, looked over at Katie who was a few feet away at an earring carousel. "The inscription is smaller than most I've seen, done in an unusual font, and part of it's illegible, due to wear." He looked into my eyes, and I felt goosebumps begin on my arms. "Do you know the story, Carla?"

"No. I looked inside but although I saw something, I wasn't sure it was even an inscription. It's so teensy."

He nodded, and looked inside the ring again. "Only one word is clear to me. *Katie*."

"What?' Katie, hearing her name, abandoned the earrings and joined us. Her eyes were wide as she registered the look on my face which was probably something like shock.

Smiling, Chip held up the ring. "Your name is engraved in here."

Katie looked at me. "But—how? Carla?"

I took her hand. "Oh, honey, here we go again. Looks like this ring was given to me so that I could deliver it to you."

Jared moaned through a smile. "I will *never* get used to this town."

Miles started to bounce in place. "Katie's getting a magic ring?"

I knelt on the floor and took his hands. "Well, she's getting a ring. But, Miles, I'll let you in on a lesson it's taken me years to learn." I caught Katie's eyes as well, to be sure she was listening. "A ring is just a ring. Love is what makes it magic."

Jared kissed the top of my head. "Amen to that."

The End...
or is it The Beginning?

From the Author

I hope you have enjoyed reading Carla Standish's story. If you are having a hard time believing the scene in Lillian's back yard, here's something to think about.

One evening years ago, my husband, son, and I had dinner in the home of an elderly lady we knew from church. I'll call her Belle. She was all alone, having lost her parents many years before, and more recently, her only sibling who had also been her best friend. Much of the time she was sad, or even bitter. But her eyes sparkled when she told us her "miracle story."

She had lost an item of jewelry on her college campus, and for years punished herself for being negligent in not taking better care of it. (The item had been given to her by a beloved family member.) Much later, when she was middle-aged and her mother was elderly, they visited the college campus. Belle brought up again her regret, and said she wished she hadn't lost that important sentimental piece. When she finished the story her mother looked down in the grass and said, "Why, here it is, Belle."

And it was! Nestled right there in the grass, waiting for Belle to reclaim it.

I didn't have any trouble believing the story, because serendipity has happened to me too. I think Belle's story was magnificent though. I'm glad that the retelling made her happy, and

I'm so grateful that she shared it with us.

Thank you for visiting Serendipity, Indiana. I hope these stories help you believe in the Magic of Love.

Magdalena

For Free Reads, Sneak Previews & backstage info, become a Newsletter Subscriber!

I love to connect with readers! Please sign up for my newsletter so we can stay in touch. Don't worry about me clogging up your email inbox—I only send an email if I have actual news to share. The sign-up form is on my website. Just type into your browser:

http://www.magdalenascott.com/p/contact.html

Also in the Serendipity, Indiana, series:

SMALL TOWN CHRISTMAS

Melissa is moving back to Serendipity, Indiana to raise her young son and run her new business—in spite of a painful past and the fact that her ex-boyfriend still lives in their hometown.

EMILY'S DREAMS

Emily Kincaid has a second chance at life, and a voice in her head that keeps nudging her along. But she can't move forward without dealing with her past.

CHRISTMAS WEDDING

Dec. 1: Jim Standish is ready—right this minute—to marry the love of his life, but Melissa Singer wants the day to be one they'll look back on forever. Planning and execution time: 25 days. Will it be possible to create the perfect Christmas Wedding?

THE BLANK BOOK

Alice Williams is surviving widowhood, but must unlock the secrets of a mysterious blank book before she can confidently step into her future with a man she's afraid to love.

THE RING

Happily-ever-after is out of the question. But in Serendipity, the Magic of Love does amazing things.

THE ROAD NOT TAKEN

Francie Standish Carrington has some tough decisions to make, and a lot of questions about a past she thought she understood.

A PIECE OF HER SOUL

Jacqueline needs a break from the constant strain of the special gift she has. But the little cottage on a quiet street isn't quite the retreat she expected, due to the presence of a handsome next door neighbor.

ONCE UPON A TIME

Taylor Kincaid has big plans for her life, and falling in love with the mysterious new shop owner in her hometown isn't one of them. Sweet romance, "coincidences" that might be more than that, and a love that survives the unthinkable come together in this new Serendipity, Indiana tale.

A COWBOY FOR CHRISTMAS

Hannah Kincaid has her eye on Jacob Hollingsworth, the handsome co-owner of Serendipity's new (and only) dude ranch. When Jacob's brother Michael shows up, everything at the Rocking H is turned on its head-- including Hannah's plans.

Magdalena's Legend, Tennessee Titles

MIDNIGHT IN LEGEND, TN

CHRISTMAS COLLISION

WHERE HER HEART IS

BUILDING A DREAM

SECOND CHANCES

CHRISTMAS CHARM

HOME FOR CHRISTMAS

UNDER THE MISTLETOE (Prequel)

THE HOLLY AND THE IVY (Prequel)